A Woman's Voice

An anthology of short stories by Ugandan women

General editor: Mary Karooro Okurut

Text editor: Violet Barungi

FEMRITE Publications
KAMPALA

FEMRITE Publications limited
P.O. Box 705
KAMPALA, Uganda.

FEMRITE-Uganda Women Writers Association-1998

First published 1998

First reprint 1999

© Uganda Women Writers Association
FERMRITE 1998

All rights reserved. No part of this publication may be reproduced, stored in retrieval system, or transmitted in any form, or by any means, electronic, mechanical, photocopying, recording or otherwise, without prior permission of FEMRITE Publications Limited.

Printed in Uganda by the Monitor Publications.

ISBN 9970 9010 3 6

Preface

FEMRITE is an indigenous voluntary and non-profit making association of Uganda Women Writers. FERMRITE's objectives, include, among others, uniting, promoting and inspiring all creative women writers and assisting in the production of their works. FERMRITE also aims at promoting a positive portray of women in the media, disseminating gender-sensitive literature in society and networking with women writers nationally and internationally.

The Association also lobbies and advocates for increased literacy programmes and intends to start book programmes for rural women.

The Literature FERMRITE intends to develop will mostly be drawn from local women writers as a way of facilitating their access to decision-making structures. There is need to have a collection of the many women writers' stories as a means of documenting women's feelings, thoughts and experiences.

A Woman's Voice — a short story anthology — will serve as a record of both the literate and semi-literate women's literature.

Mary Karooro Okurut
Chairperson, FEMRITE

Contents

Looking for my mother
by Lillian Tindyebwa 1

Mad Apio
by Susan Kiguli 16

Behind closed doors
by Lillian Barenzi 22

Joanitta's nightmare
by Hope Keshubi 28

A sacrifice for Maayi
by Ayeta Anne Wangusa 42

Santus
by Dominic Dipio 47

The last one to know
by Violet Barungi 54

Where is she?
by Philo Nabweru 67

Hidden identity
by Goretti Kyomuhendo 74

Those days in Iganga
by Regina Amollo 80

Becoming a woman
by Hilda Twongeirwe 85

The fate of an expensive wedding
by Margaret Ntakarimaze 94

Notes on the authors 97

Looking for my mother

Lillian Tindyebwa

When dawn at last broke and first rays of light started showing through the holes in the wall that served as ventilators to the tiny cell, I was already awake. When the first bird sang its song that morning, my heart, although far from being light, sang with it as I slipped from the old mat and threw away the lice infected blanket that had been the only form of bedding that I had known for the last eight years.

Eight hard years during which I often contemplated committing suicide to end my shameful existence. But each time the thought crossed my mind, I quickly put it away. I had to continue the search for my mother, and I had to find her.

Yes! I had to find that woman and make her share the eternally humiliating experience that was my life. I had to find her and haunt her like a ghost from the past. The ghost she had so carefully buried behind her when that night, twenty-eight years ago, she had carefully hidden herself under the cover of darkness and given birth to me in the pit latrine. How I would love to see the shock and consternation on her middle aged face as she realised that I was indeed the son she condemned to death; the son she never wanted to waste her time bringing up; the son who she never wished to see the light of the day. I also often told myself that as soon as I found her, I would announce my story.

Yes, the world had to see her and know that was the woman, the mother that was more cruel than a paid killer, more wicked than a witch. A mother who could not blink at the thought of throwing away an innocent three kilogram new-born baby. Her own flesh and blood! After throwing me away in that pit-latrine, did she feel any different from what she usually felt after using the latrine, I often wondered.

So, at last eight years of prison life were over. But if it had not been for this earnest desire to make that horror, in the name of my mother, pay for what she did, I would never have endured them. I felt compelled to make her understand that it was because of that indelible wound that she had inflicted on me at birth that I ended up committing that crime, a crime though accidental, was too painful for me to live with, and for which I could never find enough grace inside me to forgive myself.

And a crime which had served only to make me sink lower and lower into the bottom pit into which she had thrown me at birth. She had to be found at any cost to share with me all the bleeding wounds that made up my wretched life.

At eight o'clock, the warder came in with his mug of sugarless tea and stale bread. "I don't want it," I told him. "Better take me straight to the office where I can wait for my discharge papers."

"No, it is not possible," he answered curtly and walked out, locking the door.

"Miserable snake!" I hissed. Did he think that I would try to escape even on my last day?

Nine o'clock and he was back. "You can come out now," he said.

I brushed past him without a word and walked up the hill to where the offices were. On arrival, I was handed a black cloth bag with my name written on it. I opened it and looked inside. My clothes!

You mean they preserved those clothes for eight years? I wished they had burnt them because the sight of that jacket, that matching trouser and the expensive watch reminded me too much of him. He had bought them for me on my 20th birthday, with a card that said, 'Happy birthday son'.

But instead of being happy, I was irritated because I had come to hate my birthdays as my mind inevitably always switched back to the story of what had happened to me soon after I was born. 'What am I celebrating, anyway?' I always asked myself. 'Is it my birth or my discovery inside the pit?'

"Mr. Balaba," the Prison Superintendent's voice rang out, "don't you want to change and get discharged?"

"Oh, I do, sir," I answered quickly as I scrambled to the adjoining room to where the others were busy changing, happy and ready to go and join their families. How I envied them!

Later as I sat in the bus taking me from the prison, I remembered the last stage I had reached in my search for my mother. Oh, yes, the last stage had been my encounter with the very woman who had heard my feeble cries coming from the pit. That had been just a week before that fateful evening when my beloved, caring, and loving foster father had surprised me in my room, smoking bhang and in a bid to escape from his disapproving and disappointed stare, I had accidentally pushed him to his death. I will never forget the look of utter disbelief on his fatherly, loving face as he fell. The look was still there on his face even long after his body had become cold. And that look has haunted me all these years. I cannot say how many nights I have woken up sweating, after dreams in which I see him accusing me of ungratefulness, or simply pointing a finger at me.

Anyway, a week before that accident, I continued my secret search for my mother. I say secret, because I had made sure that my foster parents did not know what I was doing. At last I had managed to trace the woman called Nambi who had first heard my cries. She was no longer in the slum area where she had been living when I was found.

After her children had grown, she had decided to leave the city and had gone to live in a house she had constructed from years of careful saving. I came to find out all that during my search. This house was 25 miles away from the city.

She had been overwhelmed by emotion when she saw me. She did not find any difficulty in believing me. It was as if she had always known that she would see me one day. So she welcomed me. It was as if she had met a long-lost grandchild and she went to great lengths to please me and to make me feel at home. She gave me lunch and although I told her I had already eaten, she would not hear anything of it. Afterwards we relaxed like old friends and she told me the story.

***

"That morning," she started, "I had woken up with a start, yawned and stretched, wishing I didn't have to wake up so early each and every day of my life. I stared up vacantly for a few minutes then quickly jumped out of bed.

"Everyday I had to wake up at 5:00am in order to start working. My work at that time consisted of cooking food and supplying it to the market vendors at Shauri Yako. We had to start peeling early in order to fill the large saucepans with *matooke* and sweet potatoes. In fact we prepared many types of dishes, according to the customers' needs.

"After getting out of bed, I stood up in the tiny bedroom which also served as a store and pantry. I walked slowly from my bed, gropped in one corner for matches and lit my *tadooba* as it was still dark at that hour. With the *tadooba* in my hand, I walked through the curtained door into the next tiny room in which my three children were sleeping, huddled up in one corner on a mat and under one blanket. The opposite side of their room served as a kitchen. Most of the families in that slum area lived in those sort of rooms.

"I opened the door leading outside and walked out of the house cradling the frame of the candle to protect it from being blown out by the wind. In that neighborhood, I was not the only one up at that time. Already I was aware of a bit of stirring as most people here had to start their various tasks very early. I walked briskly towards the pit latrine to answer nature's call. I opened the door and immediately let out a loud cry, *a-lu-lu-lu Katonda wange he-he-he*. I stepped out again, calling out to neighbours, in between my wild screams.

"Doors were flung open as people rushed out, still rubbing sleep out of their eyes, others still in the process of dressing up, women still trying to tie their *lesos* or *busutis* around themselves and men still pulling up their shorts. Some children came out into the early morning breeze naked. Everybody was rushing anxiously to see what it could be that was making me to scream like a mad person at that hour.

"Some thought that I had perhaps come across a dangerous robber as he tried to steal the property while others, who loved juicy stories, thought that, perhaps I was screaming because I had caught my husband sneaking behind my back with a neighbour's wife or daughter.

"However, they were not prepared for what they found to be the actual cause for this early morning commotion. My face became sad and I stopped talking for sometime and then I resumed screaming. Nobody could have been prepared for those feeble cries coming from the dark depth of the pit latrine. The shock only mesmerised them for a few minutes, then there was a hullabaloo and bedlam as people frantically ran back and forth in the semi-darkness, looking for shovels, hoes, ropes, and ladders to rescue the baby while calling out to each other to hurry up.

"Sweat was dripping from their brows as half an hour later the men managed to pull out the unsightly soiled baby boy. Women were ready with basins of warm water and they quickly decided that this baby should be rushed to hospital for check-up as it looked very weak. A policeman had already been fetched while the child was being dug out and he escorted the group that took the baby to hospital."

I knew what followed. I was left at the hospital. The story had first burst out when I was 16 years old and in Form Three at a boarding school near Mukono. Up to that moment, neither my foster parents nor anybody else had ever breathed a word about the nature of my birth. I had always thought that Mr Isaiah and Mrs Karen Mweru were my real parents. They were so loving and caring that there was never any moment in my life when I would have doubted them at all.

If anything, I was always favoured as an only boy and also as the youngest child as Mr and Mrs Mweru had two daughters who were older than me. The eldest was Sophia and the second one was Sandra. They too did not know that I was not their real brother.

So that year, as soon as we came back to school for the third term, I got a shock that crippled me and blew the daylights out of my life. You see, I had this very good friend called Disan Kiti. As I learnt after I had been bullied, abused, teased and beaten by my fellow students because of my past, it had been during the previous holidays when Disan had been talking casually with his mother, in the presence of two visitors, that he had mentioned that one of his new friends was called Musa Balaba.

"Musa Balaba!" Mrs Kate Kiti had inquired again from her son, a look of surprise on her face. Disan had repeated the name for her.

" Do you know his parents?" she had asked.

"Mr and Mrs Mweru," Disan had answered simply.

"My God, you mean that boy had grown up?"

"Why is it surprising?" inquired Robinah, one of the visitors.

Mrs Kiti had first kept quiet, looking at her son, then at the visitors. Then she had said, "Would you believe it if I told I was the one who named that boy Musa Balaba?"

"You? How?" asked Disan. Her two visitors had not said anything but had stared at her questioningly.

"Well, it's a long story and a sad one too. I remember, I had just started my nursing career when some people brought in a baby boy very early one morning. They said they had just recovered him from a pit latrine.

"Mummy, what?" Disan had screamed with shock.

"Oh no," cried Robina and Aunt Cissy in unison. How terrible!"

"Yes it was terrible," Mrs Kiti had continued. "Even after treatment, the boy was so weak that the nun who was in charge of the hospital decided that we should have him baptised just in case he did not survive. At least he should go as a Christian.

"So she asked me to choose a name. That is why I chose Musa, because, as you know, Musa in the Bible was rescued from the river bank, heh? But amazingly, the boy pulled through, and we kept him at the hospital until we got a good home for him.

"Mr and Mrs Mweru had approached the hospital authorities. They wanted and boy for adoption. They had two daughters already and for some reason Mrs Mweru had been advised not to have any more children. And since they had wanted a boy so much, they decided to adopt one. And they thought Balaba was the most suitable for them, so they took him. And since that time, I had never heard of him again, until now."

The cat was out of the bag and Disan did not waste time before spreading the story. Within two weeks after the beginning of the term, I was puzzled because nobody, friends and enemies alike, wanted to associate with me.

I had been such a clever student and a popular one too. I think my enemies exploited this chance to the maximum. I would never have imagined that young people could be so cruel until that Monday morning when I entered the class.

Of course I did not yet know the story about myself. As I entered the class, I noticed that the students were standing together in little groups. I just walked casually to one group.

Then I saw them, one by one, put their hands to their noses, Michael Jackson style, and walk out quickly. Then the other groups also followed suit and as they all went out holding their noses, I heard some of them say wickedly, "Oh!, foo, foo, foo, someone is smelling like latrine here!"

I was so hurt as I stood alone in the empty classroom because everybody seemed to know what was going on except me. What was this business about smelling like a latrine? Surely I was not smelling at all.

There was nothing I could do, so I sat down at my desk and bowed my head. I was so worried about what these hostile students might do that I was relieved when the teacher came and everybody had no choice but to rush back into the classroom. That whole day I thought of nothing else. My whole mind was preoccupied in trying to find out what I had done to these students to deserve such treatment. That evening, since I did not even have anyone to talk to, I went to bed early depressed. As I was just falling into some uneasy sleep, I heard some noises, and before I could distinguish what they were, I felt my blanket being pulled off me. I looked up and quickly sat up, sensing some danger.

And standing there, towering above my bed, were four big boys known for being the biggest bullies in the school. Yes, standing there with wicked grins on their faces were Bernard, Jack, Angelo and Bill.

It was Angelo who was known to be the group leader and he spoke first, pointing at me. "Hey boy, don't pretend to be asleep, we know all about you."

"All about me?" I inquired puzzled and frightened. "And what can that be?"

"Hear how he talks 'what about me?'" said Bill, imitating my voice and thereby provoking laughter from his colleagues.

"Okay, when we say we know all about you, we mean that we know your mother threw you in a pit latrine and you were only lucky that people got you out. And your sweet mother has never been seen again. So needless to say the people you live with are your foster parents!"

With the state of mind I was already in, my first reaction was of fear and shock. The fear that this might be true. After this initial fear, my mind quickly raced and I remembered my parents. Then I quickly dismissed these bullies' statement as only meant to intimidate me for their personal pleasure. Of course there was no way I could believe that my loving parents were not actually my real parents.

As all this passed through my mind, I was relieved and happy and I even laughed as I told them that, "That is the most ridiculous accusation! Of course it is simply not true. Never."

It was Angelo again who answered with a sheer,"Is it proof that you want, heh? Then ask you best friend, Disan. His mother looked after you when you were brought to the hospital after you were retrieved from the pit latrine."

"You are lying! Anyway I won't be intimidated by your stories!" I screamed at them. Then Bernard pushed me back in bed and pulled the blanket roughly over my head and said."Okay, we'll go. You can now sleep and dream about your experiences in the depth of the earth. And of course you'll be hearing more from us." And they all walked away laughing.

The days that followed were a living hell for me. Those boys who did not join others in insulting me simply shunned me. Oh God, I felt like a leper! What was worse was that I could not bring myself to go to the teachers for help for fear of spreading the story and also probably confirming it. After three weeks of this treatment, I decided to feign sickness and obtained permission to go home.

My parents were very sorry that the students could have behaved like that, and I remembered how they tried to console me saying that what mattered was only the present and the present was that I was their son and they loved me dearly.

I understood what they were trying to tell me but somehow I failed to accept it. I was deeply hurt. It was as if suddenly someone had placed a heavy load on my back and living with it became difficult and I became depressed. I did not feel like talking to anyone and I would lock myself up in my room for hours. My sisters who had been very close to me could not understand why I was no longer talking to them, and felt hurt because of my behaviour. Eventually, my parents explained to them the reason for my depression.

Oh my sweet sisters! They really tried to help me to overcome the problem but it was as if I had lost all sense of understanding.

After a few months at home, my dear parents decided to get me a place in a nearby day school. I could not go back to my former school. No, especially after finding out that what they had said was true. There was no way I could have gone back to that humiliation. My parents also now believed that if they stayed with me all the time, they could help me, with their constant care and counselling.

I would probably have improved but after two terms at that school, the story broke out again and I could not bear the humiliation. So I refused to go back. I only went back in the third term to do exams. No wonder I never passed.

"Son, you've got to learn to face the world. You can't keep running away from all schools, you know. If you made a stand and showed these boys that you could not care less what they were saying, they would change their attitude." My father's words still rang clearly in my head. I understood what he was saying, but getting the courage to practise it was not easy.

I registered in a poor day school under a different name so that nobody would know who I was. It would probably have worked but my morale was so low and I was always living so much under the fear of being found out or of being identified that to distract myself from this constant shadow, I started hanging out with idlers and lumpens. This is how I started smoking bhang. I had more money than these people so when I was among them, I felt like a king. In this shady world, I managed to feel like somebody and once I was intoxicated with the alcohol and the drugs, I felt no fear of anybody or anything. I never even remembered who I was or whether I had any problems in life or not. I only felt happy and relaxed. It was like floating in the sky among the stars where everything felt so smooth and easy. I was well established in these habits by the time I was twenty years old. That is when that terrible accident happened. I had been with my group of lumpens one evening and we together had smoked bhang and drunk a lot of alcohol. Then I left them at 8: pm and went home.

On arrival, I did not find anybody at home. I knew my mother had gone with my sisters to see a relative, but I did not know where my father was. I sat around for about thirty minutes waiting for them. When nobody turned up I went to my room, put on music and just lay on my bed. Then after a few minutes, I got tempted to smoke the bhang that had remained. I had always been careful not to smoke at home but that day I was so tempted and like a fool, I gave in to the temptation.

I do not know whether it was because of the music, or because I was so engrossed in my world, but I did not hear my father's car as he pulled up the drive and parked in the garage. Of course he must have been attracted by the loud music and the smell of bhang could have been all over the house. He must have come to see what I was doing with myself, because I only saw him when he opened the door of my room and entered. The room was full of bad smoke and obviously I was intoxicated. Nothing could have prepared him for the state I was in.

So out of shock, he shouted, "Musa, you smoke that stuff? Throw it away at once!" I was equally shocked, probably more so to be found in that state. As he called out, I quickly got up and sat at the edge of the bed, not knowing what to do or say. Then he came towards me. I must confess this made me more frightened. So I got up and tried to push past him and get out through the door. Then he held my hand and said, "No, you stay here. You've got to explain all this."

I was not prepared to offer any explanations in the intoxicated state that I was in. So I tried to pull my hand free from his grasp. In doing so I did not realise that I was using too much force until I saw my father stagger backwards. I tried to catch him before he fell but failed. And I watched him helplessly as he fell, hitting his head on the sharp corner of a heavy coffee table that was in my room, and then finally banging it on the hard floor. I rushed to him and tried to get him up but could not. I brought cold water, poured it on him, still no response. I lifted his head up and tried to make him drink, still no response. Then as I put him down, I realised that his body was actually lifeless and I panicked. I wanted to shout but I dared not call anybody. I had to do something before my mother and my sisters came back home.

I got his car keys from the pocket. As I could not carry him, I dragged him along the floor through the corridor. Luckily for me, there was a door connecting the sitting room to the garage. I passed through it and struggled and struggled until I managed to fix him into the passenger seat. I got behind the steering wheel and drove out. I actually did not know where I was going. But I started thinking and got an idea. I had to make it look like an accident. So I drove like a man in a trance to a lonely precipice and while the motor was running, I pushed the car down the hill. I hid in the bush for a few minutes. Then I got out and started stopping cars, telling people to go and help my father who, I said was trapped in the car.

I do not know why I did such abominable things. I could not control myself. It was as if the devil himself was commanding me. And at the back of my mind, there was this terrible fear that on top of the burden I was already carrying, I had added another one. Later, of course after the post-mortem, it was discovered that the swelling on my father's head was inflicted before the car accident occurred. People became suspicious and the endless questions began. And believe you me, I could not maintain the lies. But later when I tried to tell the judge the truth, no one would believe me after failing to tell the truth from the beginning. Moreover, the story of my life had even been revealed, doubtless most people believed that I had a reason for wanting to kill my father. How, oh God, could I have wanted to kill that adorable man!

That had been eight years earlier!

* * *

My prison term was over and the bus I was travelling in from the prison ground to a halt. I got out and walked across to the taxi park to get a taxi to Nambi's place. I prayed that she would still be alive because it seemed so long ago since I had last seen her. I had asked her if there was really nobody who had any idea who my mother was. She had kept quiet for some minutes in an effort to remember.

Now, eight years later, I wondered whether if she was still alive she had kept her word. But even if she had, it was possible that she had forgotten all the information she had obtained. So I was worried and tensed up as the taxi dropped me at the roadside and I started walking slowly along the small road to her house which was about a kilometre from the main road.

My heart leapt with joy and I even managed a smile to myself as I saw her house come into view. But my smile soon waned as I imagined that she might be dead. I increased my pace as a result of my anxiety. I was almost trembling as I knocked at the door. But a few minutes later, I almost screamed with delight when I saw her. She had aged much more since I had last seen her and she did not recognise me at all. I could not blame her. She had seen me only once and now after prison, I had grown a bushy beard and of course I was much older.

After I re-introduced myself, she was happy and hugged me. I told her quickly what had happened to me. She was shocked and at the same time sorry for me. She commented that bad luck seemed to follow me everywhere. I then asked her if she had managed to find out the name of the family of my mother or not. She kept quiet for along time again, deep in thought while my heart pounded in my chest.

Then she said,"You know, my son, the situation is difficult."

"I don't expect anything to be easy," I told her slowly. "But I am used to difficulties you know."

"No, this one is a tricky situation, my son," she said. "Because your mother is now a respectable member of society. She is well educated and happily married with children. So to avoid embarrassment, she might even deny you completely."

"Have no fear of that. My will is strong. I'll manage," I told her. "After what I have endured in my life, I cannot fail to pin her down, unless of course, she is not the one."

"No, she is the one, I am very certain of that fact," said Nambi.

"Good. Then just give me the directions and I'll let you know how I fare." A few minutes later, armed with that vital information, I made my way to Entebbe on the final leg in the search for my mother.

I reached the house late in the afternoon. It must have been around five o'clock when I stood by the big high gate and banged on it. A worker came and peeped through a hole in the gate and asked me what I wanted.

"Can I please see Mrs Rebecca Kazungu? I have an urgent message for her," I said.

"What is you name please?" asked the worker.

"My name is Musa, but I don't think she knows me."

"Okay, wait there please," he said as he closed the hole again. I waited for what seemed to be a long time but was probably less than five minutes. When he came back, he just opened and told me to come in. I almost shouted with joy and excitement but I checked myself in time. So at last I was going to meet my mother! A woman I had cursed thousands of times in my life! As I walked from the gate following the worker, I tried to imagine what this woman actually looked like. 'Do I resemble her at all', I wondered. 'How would she react to my story?' Whatever reasons she might have for rejecting me, I was determined to make her accept me.

The worker led me up a few steps on to the verandah and opened the door to the sitting room. And there she was! Sitting in one corner of the beautifully furnished room with two teenage girls, one of whom, I was to learn later, was my step sister and the other a cousin. When I saw her, I was certain there and then that she was the one. But I was completely surprised to find that she was different from what I had always imagined her to be. I had imagined her to look like some pictures I had once seen in a story book of a half man half woman creature. But it was surprising to see a beautiful, composed woman sitting there sipping tea from a fine China tea cup.

As soon as our eyes met, she must have sensed that I was not just another normal visitor because I saw her shiver and I knew she felt some fear. Could it be that she had also lived all these years under the shadow of what she had done? Then she instinctively put her tea-cup down and stood up as if to prepare herself for the worst. As I looked at her, I noticed one more thing: I looked like her. I am sure she must have noticed it too from the way she stood there staring at me and shivering. She turned and said something to the girls which I could not hear. The girls got up and cleared the table and left the room. Then she came towards me. I could see she was trying hard to keep calm. She asked me to sit down and then greeted me. And then she said, "Can I help you?"

What a ridiculous question! I almost told her that it was rather too late for her to help me, that she had denied me help when I needed it most. But I decided against it because I did not want to expose my bitterness yet. My delay to reply must have worried her because she went on to say, " I understand that you have a message for me?"

"No," I answered curtly. I wished there was anyway I could mentally torture this woman first. I was even getting revolted by her soft beauty and her deceptive look of innocence.

"No?" she asked, obviously flustered.

"No. But, let's say that I'm looking for you," I said and then kept quiet again.

"Please, go on and let me know why you are looking for me."

" I'm sure you already know," I said. "Surely you know me?"

She looked at me for along time as if trying to find a trace that would convince her that I was not her son, and then in a voice that betrayed a slight tremor, she asked, "Know you? No. I don't seem to remember you at all" she added.

"That is not surprising. Not at all," I said slowly. She did not say anything. She kept staring at me. "In fact," I continued, "I would have been surprised if you had remembered me because it was a long time ago".

"A long time ago?" she asked, her voice still shaky.

"Yes," I said. "Twenty-eight years ago, to be exact."

When I said that, she looked down and placed her hand on her forehead.

"I can see your memory is slowly coming back," I added with a sneer. "I am sure that you remember the Kisenyi slum and a son that you gave birth to in the night and threw in your neighbour's pit latrine? You were so sure then that you were protected by the darkness and that I would die. No I did not die. I lived alright, although my life has been hell because of your actions. You do not know it of course, but I have just left prison this morning. Yes, I survived eight hard years of prison life because I had to find my heartless mother."

"No, no, stop there," screamed my mother. She had started crying as I was talking and through the tears she said, "No, please, I don't deserve those names. At that time, I had no choice. I had been pushed to the limits. You see, I was fifteen. My mother had taken me upcountry to stay with my aunt while going to school there. My mother always said that she did not want me growing up in the slum area where young people easily learnt bad behaviour. Little did she know that she had taken me to the leopard's lair.

"My aunt's husband, who was old enough to be my grandfather and who was a respectable member of society, had other ideas. Every time my aunt was not in the house, he would force me to have sex with him. He used even to way-lay me as I came back from school. He used to threaten me each time, saying that if I told anybody about what was happening, he would kill me.

And at that age, it was easy to believe such threats! When I got pregnant at fifteen, I told him and that day he almost killed me. He held a knife to my neck and said if I tarnished his name, he would not hesitate to use it. I cried and cried as I suffered these humiliations. I was almost going mad, but I was not going to allow this monster to succeed in destroying my life."

She stopped talking and kept on crying quietly. I was also silent. Thinking. I was beginning to realise that we had both suffered as a result of other people's actions. I can't say that my bitterness and my anger against her went away there and then. No. It was too much and I had harboured it for so long that it could not just melt away in minutes. But I felt I as if a tiny crack had been made in the icy wall that separated us.

And as for the first time I began to feel a bit of sympathy and understanding for a fifteen year old girl suffering abuse of that magnitude. And all the words I had prepared to hurl at her melted away. Instead, I felt some curiosity to know more about my father. What kind of monster could he have been? Without thinking, as if an irresistable force was driving us, my mother and I found ourselves locked into each other's arms, tears running freely down our cheeks.

Mad Apio

Susan Kiguli

To my surprise and annoyance, Biti suddenly hastened her pace.
"I thought you suggested a careful survey of these shops this morning, Biti," I called out.
Biti took a few paces back and whispered, "She is coming."
"Who?" I asked. "Oh, Mad Apio. Let her come, she is harmless," I replied lightly. "Moreover, it is not likely that she has any time to spare on a morning like this one. She must be heading for the city centre."
Sure enough Mad Apio strode past us purposefully, without as much as a nod in our direction. Biti stood very still, staring at the woman as she went past.
"Strange," said Biti. "Very strange. How can one be mad and yet so well groomed? There isn't a hair out of place. The woman seems perfectly normal without even the slightest suggestion of a murderous glint in her eyes! May be people are wrong about Apio, may be she is not mad at all," Biti insisted.
"Or may be," I said, "it is the other way round. The rest of us are mad and she is not or like someone once said, all of us, Apio inclusive, are mad and it is the degree that varies. I would rather like to think," I continued, raising my voice, "that madness is a matter of opinion rather like colour, you know. I always find it amusing when I read in those venerable textbooks about the white and black races with all those high flown theories. Why, I say, I would never call myself black, not even a colour blind one hundred and twenty year old in any state of mind would. Not that I object to being black; I am simply saying that I am not. In fact I asked my niece what colour she thought I was and she examined me for a while, looked more closely at the dark brown streaks on my right arm and the pink scar on my wrist. In that rather philosophical manner of hers, she pronounced me speckled. It made me think of that man in the Bible, I think his name was Jacob, that demanded from his master

speckled and brown cattle and goats for his wages and then through some trick made sure all the cattle and goats bore speckled and brown offspring."

"Enough," cut in a now exasperated Biti. "Are we to spend the whole morning in this one spot as you rip off story after story of brown and speckled animals! I rather think that it must be your brain that is brown and speckled. How on earth you got to that topic beats me; it was Mad Apio we were talking about! Anyhow, I am feeling hungry already! Why don't we go to that 2000 A.D. Restaurant for a bite? I would very much like to know about this Apio woman."

Mad Apio was a much discussed topic in the small town of Kati. May be because she seemed to have done things that made Kati known across the whole country. There was nothing much to see or recount about Kati except Apio of course. Story had it that she had not always been mad and that she was not native of the town. That could probably account for her rather foreign looks. She was very tall, about six feet; which was tall according to Kati standards for even though the people of Kati were not exactly midgets, they could easily pass for that. She had a high forehead and big luminous eyes. It was said that her eyes altered size according to her mood and also depending on the time of day. It was also said that at night she was indistinguishable from an owl. Come to think of it, those were very strange eyes, not at all like an owl's, if my knowledge of that bird could be trusted.

Those eyes, I can see them now very clearly, the whites were extremely white and her pupils floated around like twin beads. In fact they resembled two black beans floating in an expanse of milk. None could fail to notice those eyes. The other spectacular thing about her were her legs; they seemed to go on and on. They looked like two endless poles although watching her move, they could pass for four wheels. She used them very quickly and deftly.

We stood before the restaurant looking it over.

"Very murky," Biti pronounced.

"Yes," I cut in, "rather like the year 2000 promises to be - murky with lots of warped minds milling about. Well, I suppose things have a right to be what they are."

"Oh please," Biti pleaded, "do not start on that rights issue of yours, not now at least. Let us sit and have a rest from this unbearable heat and then talk about Apio."

Certainly the subject of Mad Apio loomed large on Biti's mind. She was curious and wanted to know more to fit in the pieces of this puzzle called Apio.

We settled down at a table nearest the door in a bid to catch some fresh air. Fans were unheard of in this part of the world but no one fainted for lack of them, so they were not mentioned or bought. It was rumoured that growing up in the hot sun made one oblivious of petty discomforts and that it conditioned one to accept even the heaviest of burdens as if it were a light load. It seemed that we had not got enough of the sun's heat because we were soon arguing with the waitress about unboiled water and unprotected wells. The woman's pupils dilated in surprise as if she thought we would soon be demanding to inspect the kitchen. All the same she assured us that the water was boiled and kept in clean pots as she served passion fruit juice to us.

Biti toyed with her mug and said, "Tell me about Apio, we do not have much time to spare. Why does everyone think she is mad anyway?"

I searched Biti's face to make sure she was serious. I then asked "Do you mean to tell me, Biti, that you do not know what distinguishes a mad person from the normal? Anyway, where do you want me to begin? I could spend a fortnight on Apio's story.

"I hear it started with her father who on seeing her peculiar eyes named her 'Bell eyes'. He was convinced that his daughter's eyes said more than her mouth. You know for a fact how one's name decides one's fate in many ways. Thus Apio's eyes have been the centre of many a story. Well, since we have limited time, I will just tell you the highlights of the woman's life.

"I will start with the part when she was at university. Did you know she did a bachelors of languages or rather half of it! She was discontinued before she completed the degree. That is a story on its own and I will not deal with it here. But anyway, the story goes that Apio, who was already considered odd, became increasingly strange. She was, as a consequence, involved in some incidents that almost made her a legend. The most entertaining one was when she once attended a graduation dance, and after a while went outside to catch some air. She ended up falling in an uncovered septic tank. It is said that half of her was covered in sewage but she never called for help. No one was even sure of how she got out of such a deep hole.

"The story got round and excited all the boys who started calling her 'Septic Apio'. One particular boy, a well known bully, taunted her about this so much that Apio decided to fix him. She called him to a wrestling match and made sure that all the students got to know about it. The boy declined giving the reason that it was not proper to fight a woman. 'If you will not fight a woman, why then do you call this woman names?' she challenged. 'Alright, I will not fight with you, I will beat you up.'

True to her word, she sprang onto the boy in the quadrangle of his hall of residence and gave him a thorough whipping. The other boys just stood around cheering her on and chanting, 'Apio, our man, you are tough'. After this incident, the nickname was never heard of again."

By this time Biti was laughing so much that people kept looking in our direction, wondering what was happening. "Is that why she was expelled then?" asked Biti amidst gasps of laughter.

"No, she was not expelled for beating up Bull, as the boy was known. She was discontinued for leading a strike in her second year. Many people agreed that the expulsion was unjustified but the question of injustice is a thorn in the flesh in this part of the globe.

"The story goes that Apio led the students strike that followed the removal of their maintenance allowances. Her policy, as one of the student leaders, was that if students' allowances had to go, an alternative ought to be put into place. I am sure you have ever heard of that strike and also heard that the government sent in soldiers to quell it? When the soldiers went to the campus, they broke into the students residences, shooting and beating anyone in sight.

"It is said that a contingent of soldiers were went to Apio's room. She refused to open for them so they broke down the door. There was Apio standing in the middle of the room, brandishing a big knife. The soldiers were under strict instructions to take her to their boss uninjured but Apio was not prepared to go without a fight. The leader pleaded with her to no avail. She told them that since they had gone to her with their guns, she would also talk to them with her knife. The soldiers left. You have probably heard the kind of stories that surrounded that incident. After the strike was quelled, with fifty students dead and countless ones injured or raped, Apio was expelled for leading the strike. I do not know exactly what followed after that. All I know is that she ended up here and married the late Sati.

"It is widely believed that Sati was as mad as Apio. It is said that during the last presidential elections, Sati and Apio got the Boss' campaign posters and plastered them outside their latrine. The Boss' local campaign manager inevitably inquired into the matter. Those two calmly told him that everything has its place in life and that as far as they were concerned, what the human body rejected rightly deserved to rest in latrines and other similar places. They were both detained at the maximum prison. I will not tell you what Sati did there, it is beside the point. Suffice to say that the Boss ordered their release and recommended that they be transferred to the hospital for the insane.

"I suppose we better leave now, we seem to have overstayed our welcome, the waitress is looking at us quite impatiently."

"No please," pleaded Biti. "Let's order lunch so that you can tell me the incidents following Sati's death."

"Biti, are you going to write Mad Apio's biography or what?" I asked.

"No. I am just interested and since you know so much about her, why shouldn't I use the opportunity to learn as well," Biti interjected.

The waitress brought us u*gali* and beans. I looked at it dispassionately. The *ugali* was not quite the right colour and the beans were decorated with weevil holes. This is a matter of paying cheaply for one's death, I thought. When will our people learn to provide good service to all, the poor inclusive? It was an unvoiced agreement among these people that the ones with little money could be served anything under heaven, including the hind parts of rats in their soup, I thought. But loudly, I continued the story.

"You must have heard," I told Biti "that Sati took ill suddenly and died as suddenly?"

"Yes, it was sad, wasn't it? I hear those two were inseparable and I think it is better to be two mad people than one mad woman with two little children," Biti cut in.

"Well, Sati died and it is rumoured that Apio's madness reached its height then. First of all, at the wake, that woman never raised the traditional wail, actually she did not even cry at all. She sat in the corner, silently watching others weep. She fixed her eyes in silence on all the women who were tearing their hair in sorrow and stayed very quiet. Of course people branded her a witch and others confirmed her madness. She sat there with all the keys to the rooms in the house on a knot on her wrist and so the relative had to find their own beddings and utensils."

"But wasn't she right?" Biti questioned. "You know as well as I do that people use this opportunity to strip the bereaved of even the little property they possess."

"That is not it," I told her excitedly. "Just listen to me, young woman. After the burial the elders of the clan came back to the house. They demanded the land title and also informed Apio that she would have to leave their son's house. She listened patiently as Sati's eldest brother told her that they were going to make a list of his brother's property and see how it would be distributed and that the two daughters were her responsibility. He even said that the sooner she left with them the better. The house was for Sati's heir who happened to be that man's son. Mad Apio listened calmly, turned her eyes on her father-in-law as if she were seeing him for the first time. She then excused herself, got her two daughters, locked them in a room and went to her bedroom where she stripped herself naked. She then came back to the front room. She turned slowly and pointed at her bottom saying, 'This was one of your son's favourite possessions, so write it down, go ahead, write.' There was a stampede as all the elders fled except Sati's old father who had fainted. His sons came back and dragged him out. Mad Apio had done it! It was taboo to even look your father-in-law in the eye but to show your nakedness was something new to Kati. There was no ruling on that. It was decided that the woman was mad and should be left alone. No one tampers with Mad Apio anymore, not even the village councils.

"Talk about the devil, there she comes again. She must be through with her morning debate. She, being mad, has the privilege of debating with anyone mad enough to listen to her on all issues concerning dictators, corrupt leaders and guerilla movements. She does this in the city square. Nobody minds Apio, at least the authorities are not threatened by her because she is mad."

" She must be," Biti conceded.

Behind closed doors

Lillian Barenzi

Right now, there are seven of us, all jazzed up and painted, crammed into this little car on our way to crash a party. A birthday party no less; for sure Kampala elite will jump at any chance to retain their places among the list of *Who's Who*.

That is partly why were are going; no *Who's Who* would be complete without us. At least that's the way we've been led to believe. From the day we all made our way through the wrought iron gates of the University two years ago, we've been top on the list of 'crucial invitees'. No party starts without us.

Until recently, that is. Blame it on the freshers, blame it on Kate's drunken obscenities or Joan's prowess with other ladies' men. Something or someone certainly put a blight on our popularity. But we fixed that like we do most things; we go when they invite, we crash when they don't. And the rest of you go suck a lemon.

A bottle of some dubious concoction was passing back and forth in the car. Kate, as usual, was already under the influence. Her buddy, Ginny, was well on the way as well. The two had a bond that went deeper than our general camaraderie.

"Sisters," Joan screamed from the back, "am I going to get lots of balls tonight or what?" We fell about laughing like banshees.

Kate started counting, "... two, four, six.." We carried on, screaming uncontrollably. The driver of the white rental sped by the Golf course obviously enjoying himself. Rhona's bare thighs were spread on both sides of the gear shift, her mini riding to China. Squashed beside her in the little bucket seat, Monica hunched by the dashboard protecting her wild coiffure from the wind.

Now we were singing along with the stereo. It was one of Chaka Demus and Pliers' ragga hits that had taken Uganda by storm. In the back seat we lolled about, already high on the night, the life, sure that tomorrow would never come.

Sara was giving directions. The car turned into the affluent neighborhood of Tank Hill and strained up the hill, past floodlit compounds and tall gates with terse warnings about biting dogs. I could feel it, this was going to be a good one. Lots of good food, lots of booze. We toned down the noise when Sara pointed at a red gate besieged by neat cars. "Ooh," Joan gasped, pretending to shiver with anticipation. "Men, men, here I come." We giggled as we eased out of the car and hurriedly paid the driver.

We clip-clopped up the driveway confidently; nodding curtly to the gateman who seemed more bored than watchful. "He didn't ask for invitation cards," I whispered to Sara, almost accusingly. We all stopped for a mini conference on the verandah. God forbid that we were in the wrong place. Sara swore that she had been told by a reliable source, a male friend of her sister's, and his car was among those outside the drive.

Kate stamped a drunken foot impatiently. "Let's go in then, after all, what can they do to us?" she asked philosophically. "If there is a mistake, we ask for a ride and go dancing. We don't lose anything." Before we could argue, a clean shaven man in short sleeves and dark pants stepped out of the house.

"Come in, ladies, the party is in the house not here." Nobody could argue with that and we started to sidle past him into the house; Kate first, then Ginny, Rhona, Sara, myself, Monica and Joan. As we all stepped into the dim lit living room, we learnt two things. We were the only women present and none of the men was a day younger than thirty-five. There were about eleven of them. Most of them shaved bald, obviously well to do and probably married. Once we realized this, we stood aghast, almost like silly sheep. Sara took the plunge and went to say hello the only man she knew; the aforementioned sister's friend.

He in turn introduced her around and then turned to us, now perched precariously on low love seats spread strategically all over the enormous room. Sara called out our names, starting with mine, Irene, Kate, Joan etc.. all the way down the line. That was our cue to mingle, which most of us did with aplomb.

I couldn't help but notice the way their handshakes seemed to linger and the way their eyes devoured whatever skin was unconcealed, and there was plenty of that. Between us all, we managed a cool number of five outfits that could be ruled as indecent and two more none of us would want our parents to see us in. We hadn't planned on being the only flesh at the feast though.

The bar was impressive. One of the men said he was a self-appointed barman and amidst much good natured teasing took our orders. Now this was familiar ground and we went for it with gusto. Kate was soon settled with her favorite lager and the rest of us reclined with cocktails and relaxed enough to look around for the first time.

The room was done in greens and browns, with pretty lampshades and lots of soft rugs. The men spoke slowly, and made only the most gentlemanly jokes. One of them was introduced as the Reverend and he went about his business in a deft, pious manner. The rest of them seemed to be ordinary run-of-the-mill personalities, more likely engaged in some business of some sort. A few of them had to have lived abroad before; they were too different from what we usually got.

Someone brought out a cake, already sliced. Apparently they had dispensed with the ceremony before we arrived. And I still didn't know whose birthday it was. Just as I picked up the courage to ask someone, I noticed one of the guys was spooning cake into Kate's mouth with his little finger. Holy smoke, suddenly I noticed everybody was paired up.

Signaling to Sara, I made my way across sprawling bodies into a room done up in blue with a blue light. Whoever lives here must be kinky for sure. Sara opened the door abruptly and asked what was wrong. I noticed she slurred her words and the zip on the front of her orange tank top was half-way undone.

"What is going on?" I asked urgently.

"Why, aren't you having fun?" was the innocent reply.

"I was, but can't you see something funny is going on?"

"We can't leave now, we can't!" Sara said, almost hysterical. "Besides, I think his holiness, the Reverend, likes you," she added slyly.

I refused to budge. The thought of eating cake off the Reverend's little finger filled me with revulsion for some reason. I was starting to suspect some sort of set up. Grabbing Sara by the shoulders, I gave her a little shake and asked about her so-called sister's friend. "What exactly did Gilbert say when he told you about the party?" I asked her. Suddenly it was of absolute importance that I know.

"Well...," she started. I gave her another shake, more viciously.

"He said a friend of his was having a birthday party and that I could come along with a few friends. That's all," she finished defensively.

But I wasn't finished. "Did he say how many?"

"He said about five or six. What's wrong with you?"

Before I could reply, the door opened and Gilbert stood there with an insolent grin on his round face. "We were starting to get worried about you girls," he rasped, reaching for Sara and yanking her out of my grasp. "You better come out too, someone is getting pretty lonely," he winked at me.

I returned to a living room that was almost empty. Looking around in alarm, I found the Reverend sitting as still as a sphinx in one of the dimly lit corners. Fixing his inscrutable eyes on me, he motioned for me to join him. My glass had been moved as well. Feigning a nonchalance I did not feel, I sat down and asked where everybody was.

"I'll show you in a minute," was all he said.

Apart from one guy swigging from a bottle at the bar, and two or three others I could hear out on the balcony, there was no evidence of my company. All of a sudden I was very much afraid. This time for sure, we wouldn't by laughing when we went over the details.

The Reverend abruptly put down his glass of red port and stood before me. He was a big man, gone soft around the edges, but still big enough to be frightening. At least I was frightened. I looked up inquiringly and I wasn't reassured by what I saw.

He put out a massive hand and when I ignored it, he took my glass firmly in one hand and pulled me off the settee with another. By now I was panicking, but I took some comfort from the presence of the guy sitting at the bar. Surely, nothing bad could happen to me while he was there.

"Where are you taking me?" I asked, trying not to sound hysterical. Without bothering to respond, the Reverend started up the carpeted stairs with me in tow. The bloke at the bar could have been cut out of ice for all the notice he took of us. I decided to save my energy for later. I hoped to God I wouldn't need it.

At the top of the stairs I realised we were heading for one of the closed doors along the corridor. By now he was literally dragging me along as I held onto anything, art objects, furniture, to stop him. I held onto a door knob for a bit and I thought I heard Kate scream. I began to fight in earnest. I bit and scratched at the hand that held me, shouting loudly for help.

We could have been in a twilight zone for all the response I got. The corridor remained cold and eerie, guarding, God knows what secrets behind its closed doors. The room at the end was humongous; a giant bed surrounded by polished wooden furniture; stools, figurines, and large paintings. He flung me onto the bed and closed the door behind him.

"Take them off," the Reverend said quietly.

He watched me cowering on the other side, and repeated his insane request. "Take your clothes off and this will take a short time. Don't make me come and take them off because you won't have anything to wear back to school or wherever you girls came from."

I started thinking fast. I had to. Even though my head felt woozy and empty. They must have spiked our drinks, I realized suddenly. And I was angry enough to do what I had to do. I stood up slowly and started unbuttoning my shirt.

"You don't use condoms, I hope," I said casually. He looked shocked. I continued, "It has never mattered to me either way, but I thought you should know I have always done it live." I paused surreptitiously to glance at him.

He was astounded. "You are trying to scare me," he blustered obviously disconcerted at my candor.

"No, I am not. I am just trying to have fun like I always do. As long as there are no condoms, I am game," I finished my little speech as I undid the last of the little buttons on my skimpy shirt.

There was an imperceptible shift in the wind. He was not prepared to risk it. I could almost see his mind working. It was a risky bet as far as I was concerned. Without a condom, he most certainly caught AIDS. Using one forcefully almost certainly meant damaging the condom and ending up a dead man. I held my breath even as I reached for the waistband of my hot pants.

"Don't bother," he barked roughly. "Put on your clothes and get the hell out of my house." I thought 'gladly', but I didn't move. He walked back to the door and opened it.

"I am not leaving without my friends," I said quietly. All the while I wanted to yell, "You despicable dog, you pevert, you." But I could not. He stalked away and I heard him knocking on several doors along the corridor. When I heard voices, I ventured out of the bedroom.

There were my buddies, in all states of *deshabille*, stumbling drunkenly down the stairs. I joined them, though none of us spoke. We couldn't get out of the den of iniquity fast enough. A car with a driver purred in the driveway and we trooped into it without a fuss. Only the Reverend stood on the verandah to watch us off; no one waved. The gates swung open and we sped off.

None of us said a word; not even as we crept into our respective beds back at the hostel. Personally, I was not ready to hear about anyone's experience behind those closed doors. Suffice to say the unpleasantness would be too galling.

Joanitta's nightmare

Hope Keshubi

Sex is vital in human life and relationships and as a result of this, there are so many taboos, stories and myths from different religions and cultures about sex that have made many young people very curious about it. This curiosity has led some of them into some problems as was the case with Joanitta and Jackson.

Joanitta and Jackson first met during the inter-school drama festival where they both played the lead characters in the respective school dramas. They had put in a lot of effort and they played their roles so well that when they were declared best actor and best actress, the audience gave them a wild clapping of hands, a deserving gesture of acknowledgement and total agreement with the judges. It was at this moment that their eyes actually met for the first time. And as if drawn together by an irresistible force, they moved towards each other and found themselves locked together in a tight embrace, oblivious of the audience cheering wildly.

The moment their bodies touched, their hormones were let loose and the hidden feelings, that had up till now never had cause to stir, came into motion. It was then they discovered that they were no longer the boy and girl . They were man and woman, ready to explore the secrets of life.

That was how it had all started for them. Right from the start, it had been love at first sight or was it at first contact? It was a love that was deep and compelling; a love endless and unending. That night they had gone for a walk and the weather had favoured their new found love. The moon lit the night, giving it a romantic feel. And Joanitta, lying on her back with Jackson's arm cushioning her head, could not help but feel that she had tumbled on the biggest miracle of her life — a boy who seemed to make her feel that she was truly a woman.

Jackson, on his part, could not help the sensation that the electric shocks that resulted from his body touching Joanitta's was sending down his groin and he could not bring himself to resist the urge to pull her closer. From what he had read, he knew what was happening to him. But he could not help the fear that gripped him on how he was expected to handle the situation. He plucked some courage and started caressing Joanitta. At first his hands lacked the confidence which they later gained, tickling her to a pleasure she had never experienced in all her life before. Then followed a long deep kiss that nearly left both of them breathless.

Before reason had returned to them, emotion had got hold of them and they could not stop to think what they were doing. Joanitta's knickers were off and Jackson had slid into her as carefully and smoothly as he could make it, surprising himself on how one could do such a delicate thing so successfully on the very first attempt. He had never taken a woman in all his life. But he had read a lot about sex in romance books and knew that breaking the hymen could cause a girl a lot of pain. And he could not think of hurting Joanitta in any way because he had began to feel for her in a very special way. They had never dreamt of what it meant to have pleasurable sex. They had been led to imagine that sex resulted in pain and frustration. What surprised them most was how they reached the heights of pleasure in unison.

That night, after kissing each other good night, they parted company reluctantly after exchanging addresses and promising to write to each other everyday. Two days after the drama and life festivals, Joanitta received a letter. She tore it open with trembling hands and a pounding heart as if her heart had waged war on her rib-cage. And it was equally sweet for it had the best news she had ever read in a letter.

Sweet J,
How have you been since we were last together?
I cannot claim to have been very well myself. The memories of that night keep me company every passing second. During the day, classes drag on and I hardly follow what the teachers are trying to make us learn. Every night I try to sleep, you invade the solitude of my bed, making it impossible for me to sleep. You have began to possess me like no girl has ever done before, so much so that I cannot eat nor sleep. The effect you have on me is just magical — it drains energy out of me. I don't think I can wait ... We somehow have to meet before we beak off for our Christmas holiday.

I picture your smooth skin as it shone smoothly in the moonlight that night. I love you very much, Joanitta. For some reason I cannot explain, your presence, your touch, your voice, inspire me. My words when I speak to you are terribly inspired, they are full of myself. They are like songs. Joanitta, a moment comes, and it comes only once in the life of a young woman, when, like you, she is in the peak of her prime.

At this moment she is full like the full-blown rose, fragrant and lovely to behold. And bees and other insects rush to her: some to steal the pollen, others merely to eat away the petals and the leaves. But unlike the rose, the young woman must select only one man to suck her nectar. This is your moment of decision, my beloved, Joanitta.

During this crisis, you must make a crucial, historic decision. I do not envy a young woman in your situation because the entire issue is bedevilled by the fact that she hardly knows her would-be husband. No one knows another until they have lived together for some period, and even then, never completely. The decision is, therefore, a gamble, a risk. A fatal one, should a wrong choice be made, for never again will this moment in your life return to you! It is like being born. A person can only be born once, unless of course, you are a Christian! Unfortunately, love is never based entirely on reason and logic. Feelings, belief, prejudices, rumours, shyness ... all enter into it. It is because of this that I watch you with sympathy, at the cross-road of your life. Beautiful, lively, intelligent, fabulous, trying to select which road to follow, a decision which should be taken in a cool frame of mind, since it will permanently, irrevocably, affect your entire future — the forty or so years ahead of you.

Woman of my bosom, Joanitta, I want you to be my wife. Not merely to be a house-wife. I want a vigorous life-partner for whom the sky will be the limit. Your marriage should not be a kind of vegetable life, but an adventurous. Hot, hard, difficult but rewarding. But to succeed in life, you must believe in life; you must believe in yourself, your abilities and capabilities. And these you have in plenty.

Joanitta, I dream of times when we shall live together as husband and wife. Live together never ever to be parted — not even in death. And I know deep down in my heart that I'm blessed to have *you as my love. My eyes are blinded by your dazzling beauty and will never lovingly look at another girl. They will devour you lovingly all the days of our lives.*

Sweetheart, please write and tell me when we can meet. Pour out all the sweet contents of your heart to me, my lovely beauty.

Love,

J

That afternoon, all the teachers who came to her class noticed that Joanitta was absent-minded and wondered what was happening to her. She was a particularly brilliant girl and never missed contributing to the class discussion. But the whole of that afternoon she had spent fondling Jackson's letter and trying to formulate a reply. So none was happier than her when the drum to announce the end of the last lesson was sounded. Her friends noticed her absence from the dance practice that evening but she did not seem to give a damn as she sat in the school orchard reading and re-reading Jackson's letter. She could have read it a hundred times and she would have continued reading it over and over again if she had not been interrupted by the bell announcing supper.

That night after supper, she bought a special light blue writing pad on which was inscribed 'I love you with all my heart'. And during prep time, in her neat round hand-writing, she wrote Jackson her first love letter, a letter from the bottom-most part of her heart.

My own darling, J,

Since my eyes alighted on your face, I have discovered a part of myself that I had never imagined I had the capacity to possess. Gently like a dove, you entered my treasure house, and there you nest, giving me the comfort and feeling of complete and total happiness.

I don't think I can ever find the words to clearly express the fire that you have lit in me — a low glowing fire that warms me even when we are miles apart. A fire whose glow has made me see who I am.

Sweetheart, yes, I am willing to marry you, to share the rest of my life with you. Yes, I would want to start a new life with you. A life hot, hard, difficult but rewarding. A life where the sky will be the limit.

But you know as well as I do that this is a critical decision as I try to select the road to follow. A decision which I need to take when I'm in a cool frame of mind. Sweetheart, this decision will be historical. It is permanent, irrevocable and will affect our entire lives.

Darling, let us be calm and patient. Let us not rush things. And talking about our meeting, I cannot see a possibility of our meeting before the holiday without our having to take a French leave from school. You know I love you so much that I cannot afford to lose you by doing anything silly: anything that could be avoided. Please, let us not let emotion override reason. Please, please, let us wait. Wherever you are, whatever you do, always remember, I love you so much, darling.

Kiss the second finger of your left hand for me.
Take good care of yourself.
Your love,
J

All this had been at the beginning of their third term. But all had not gone well for them. Towards the end of the term, as Joanitta and Jackson were eagerly counting the days towards the Christmas holiday, the divine-priestess' eyes of the matron noted that Joanitta's lower abdomen was beginning to bulge.

A week before the holiday, Joanitta was summoned to the headmistress' office.

"Joanitta, do you know why I have called you here today?" the headmistress asked her.

Joanitta's heart skipped a beat or two but she still managed to answer as calmly as she could, "No, Madam."

"This term, you performed very well at the drama festival and brought honour and fame to this school. We all appreciate that."

"Thank you, Madam."

"But since that festival, the teachers have noticed that you have not been very active in class and that is very disappointing because you used to be a very active, lively student. A student whom all of us believed was a potential distinction candidate. What has suddenly happened to you, Joanitta?"

Did this woman surely expect me to confide in her my love relationship with Jackson? Joanitta thought. No. I just can't. How can I when I have even refused to confide it in my best friend, Sarah? It is a matter strictly between me and Jackson. It is not for public consumption. "I have been having severe headaches for some time, Madam," she finally said.

"Have you informed the matron about them?

"No, Madam. I have been using headex to clear the pain."

"Is that all that has been disturbing you?"

"I have also been feeling very dizzy in the mornings. I feel like I am going to vomit and in fact I sometimes actually vomit."

"When did you last have your period, Joanitta?" the headmistress asked in a motherly tone, fondly putting her arms around the girl's shoulders.

Joanitta rewound the time back three months and replayed it. She suddenly realised that she had skipped her periods in the last three months.

"What has my periods got to do with how I feel, Madam?"

"When did you last have it, Joanitta?"

"Three months ago."

"Oh dear, dear!" the headmistress moaned unconsciously.

"What does that mean, Madam?" Joanitta asked innocently.

"Never mind, girl. Everything will be all right," the headmistress said in a consoling voice.

She poured Joanitta a cup of tea from a giant flask and gave her some cakes. She then went to the telephone and asked for the extension to the matron's house. Before Joanitta had finished her cup of tea, the matron had arrived in the office. She exchanged a meaningful look with the headmistress as she greeted her politely, and then Joanitta in a motherly tone.

After taking her cup of tea, Joanitta was told to lie down on her back, on the coach in the corner of the headmistress' office. The matron then gently touched the lower part of her abdomen for sometime before she nodded to the headmistress. The headmistress could not hide the tears that suddenly welled up within her. Why was life always unfair to the best of the girls? What was it that the school system had failed to do to prepare them for life? What was it that the parents were failing to do?

This should not have happened to such a brilliant, innocent girl like Joanitta. To hide the tears that were now freely rolling down her face, she turned to look through the window, and pretended to be watching the blooming flowers in the garden.

There were flowers of different shapes and colours. Flowers beckoning the insects to suck their nectar. Now they were blooming but soon they would begin to fade. And she saw Joanitta as one of these flowers. Which insect had pollinated Joanitta? She was convinced that it must have been a single pollinator for she knew that Joanitta was not a promiscuous girl. And if this mushroom had not broken out of the anthill into the open, she would have vouched for Joanitta's virginity.

She turned round and whispered something into the matron's ear. The matron nodded and walked out of the office, with a forlorn look on her face.

"Joanitta, you are expecting a child," the headmistress finally announced. And when Joanitta did not respond, she asked, "Did you hear me, Joanitta? You are pregnant," she added as she moved closer, and once again placed her loving arms around Joanitta's shoulders.

"Yes, I did, Madam. But I just don't know whether to believe it or not."

"What do you mean, child?"

"Is it possible to get pregnant the first time one has sex?"

"I thought so," the headmistress said more to herself than to Joanitta.

"What did you say, Madam?"

"Never mind what I said, child but yes, it is possible. Very possible."

"Then I have no reason not to believe what you have just told me."

Pregnancy takes most girls by surprise because in most cases, they have not planned for it. They are not ready to handle the strain of pregnancy or the criticism of society. They are no longer regarded as children yet they are not adults and cannot fit in society. That is why many of them abandon their children or are forced to marry without a choice. If they are in school, they drop out of school with no hope for the future. And Joanitta was just trying to figure out what was going to happen to her when the headmistress interfered with her train of thought.

"If I had a way, I would avoid taking you home to your parents. But then the school regulations say that every girl who gets pregnant must be taken back to her parents. So, I will have to do just that immediately the matron packs your things and brings them here," she said gently, squeezing Joanitta's shoulder. "Do you love the father of the baby you are carrying?"

"I don't love anyone else more than him," Joanitta answered without hesitation.

"It makes the situation better, Joanitta, for then, you will face it with love and not with bitterness and hate."

Before taking her home, the headmistress told Joanitta that many girls who get pregnant while at school think of abortion at one time or another.

"What is abortion?" Joanitta had asked.

"The removal of the child from the mother's womb before the baby can lead a life on its own," the headmistress explained before continuing to explain why Joanitta should not think of an abortion. She explained that in this country, abortion is illegal and that because of this, the methods commonly used to carry out abortions are crude, unhygienic and hurried. This is dangerous to both the baby and the mother and could easily result into death.

She went on to tell her that when the baby is removed by sharp instruments, a lot of bleeding occurs as a result of injury to the mouth of the womb or to the uterus itself. Also when a baby is removed, pieces of the placenta can easily remain in the uterus and will bleed endlessly. The girl can bleed to death, especially if she does not seek medical attention. Then she explained how because of the unhygienic conditions under which abortions are carried out in this country, there is a high chance of infection. That this infection may spread to the tubes and ovaries and if the tubes and uterus are not treated, scar tissue may form in the tubes. In some cases, the tubes and uterus must be removed and then the girl will be unable to have a baby in future.

All sorts of thoughts went through Joanitta's mind in quick succession as the headmistress drove her the scores of miles to her home. Joanitta had always admired this caring and loving headmistress but today her admiration for her increased as she carefully negotiated the dangerous bends on this winding mountainous road. The headmistress and matron had promised to keep it to themselves about why she was suddenly leaving the school. Joanitta was to have her child and then come back and continue with schooling. She was such a promising student that they could not afford to see her future go up in ruins. And not once had they uttered any angry words. They had acted with deep concern and understanding. It was as if in a way they had considered themselves partly responsible for what had happened to her. But her admiration for this great lady was marred by thoughts of how her parents would receive the news.

She was not as worried about her mother as she was about her father, for she could not put anything beyond him. He was a loving and caring father but he was over protective of his children. And he had a fiery temper which sometimes made her think that children would be better off if they had a choice in their parents. She knew that her mother also had moments of wishing that if her parents had given her a way, she would not have had him for a husband. And her fears came to pass.

When a young girl gets pregnant, people in the community react in different ways and in the majority of cases, these reactions are not friendly and are usually not helpful. Every parent feels hurt and betrayed when their daughter gets pregnant outside marriage. Their ability as good parents is questioned by society. Many focus on the shame it brings them as parents and their wasted resources in sending the girl to school. They feel let down and look at the girl as a guilty person and them as the wronged. The girl is not given a chance to explain what happened and in the end she is isolated from her parents.

And the case was not much different for Joanitta. Soon after the headmistress had driven off, Joanitta's father, having promised her that they would be sympathetic with her, clearly demonstrated his meaning of what being sympathetic was. He dashed to the bedroom and grabbed his hunting spear. On his way from the bedroom, he stormed to the kitchen and grabbed Joanitta's mother with his free hand and dragged her to the sitting room. He roughly called out, "Joanitta, come to the sitting room immediately!" When Joanitta delayed he shouted, "Come out of that room or else I will be forced to come and bring you out myself."

"Joanitta, please hurry. I don't want to provoke your father to use his fists on both of us," her mother pleaded.

"Shut up, woman! It is all your fault that she has gone and got herself pregnant!" he roared at her.

"Baba, you know very well that I do not tell my girls to become pregnant," she said in defence.

"Yes, but you should have taught her how not to get pregnant," he said heatedly. "Anyway, I should have known when I married you that such things would happen. After all, didn't five of your seven sisters get pregnant before marriage?"

"Joanitta, come out of there before your father's eyes get red!"

Joanitta finally dragged herself out of the refuge of her bedroom to face her father's wrath. He grabbed her and threw her onto the ground, face upwards and placed the sharp end of his spear shaft on her belly. "If you don't want me to use this spear to rip your stomach open and remove this unwanted bastard, name the man responsible so that I can demonstrate the effective use of my spear on him!" But threaten as he did, Joanitta dared not tell them who was responsible for her pregnancy. She loved him so much that she did not want to involve him in this family warfare.

That night before her father went to drink, he warned both mother and daughter that they would have to tell him the unwanted father of his unwanted grandchild. If they were not prepared to do it on their own, he was going to beat it out of them. So, the moment he left home in the evening, Joanitta's mother smuggled her out of the village to one of her distant cousin's home with a plea that she should look after her until her time came. She was convinced that when the baby arrived, it would soften her husband's heart.

* * *

The six months that followed were a nightmare in Joanitta's life. To pay for the inconvenience she had brought to her aunt, she had to labour on the farm and carry out all the household chores. There was nothing for nothing and she knew well enough not to complain.

Everyday before the crack of dawn, she would get up before every other person in the home. She would transfer the goats from the goat pen and tether them under the big mango tree. She would remove the goat droppings and keep them for use later.

She would then go to the well and fetch water. She would light the fire and put on the water for breakfast. As she waited for the water to boil, she would be grinding the millet for making breakfast. Breakfast ready, she would then wash the plates and saucepans used the previous night.

She would go to the gardens and work up to about noon when she would go home in time to prepare lunch for the family. She would then release the goats to go grazing. Lunch ready, she would go back to the gardens and work till dusk when she would drag herself home, no one seeming to care about her condition.

She would go to the well for water, wash the plates and saucepans used at lunch, and prepare the food for supper. Once supper was on the fire, she would tether the goats in the goat pen and bathe the children. She would then serve supper and go to sleep.

This would happen daily from Monday to Friday. On Saturday, she would wake up at the crack of dawn and take the saucepans and dirty clothes to the well for general cleaning. She would scrub the saucepans with river sand till she saw her reflection in them. She would then carry the saucepans packed in a basket, on top of the clothes in a big basin on her head and a jerry can of water in her hands.

After preparing and serving breakfast, she would go back to the river and collect clay soil. This she would mix with the goats droppings she had collected over the week and mix them into a paste. She would use this paste for smearing the kitchen and the latrine floors. She would then prepare and serve lunch. After lunch, she would mend the latrine covers if it was necessary and collect soft leaves for use after the long call. She would also make sure that the stand for holding these leaves was good enough. This done, she would collect dry banana leaves and smoke the pit latrine.

That done, she would then collect millet from the granary and put it on the winnowing tray. She would thresh it, winnow out the chaff and using dry banana leaves, she would roast it. After that, she would pound the millet, then winnow it, thoroughly removing stones and other impurities. The sorting done, she would pound split and dried cassava and mix it with the millet. She would then go to the well and fetch water, wash the plates and saucepans used at lunch and prepare supper.

It was like this week after week until her time came. And when the arrival time for the baby came, Joanitta was as ill-prepared for it as she had been for its conception and her pregnancy announcement. This made her have a very difficult delivery in which she nearly lost her life.

She always thought about her headmistress and remembered her promise that she could resume schooling after weaning her child. But with whom would she leave her lovely baby girl if she decided to go back to school? Her aunt's husband was already beginning to look at her child as an extra burden on him, and she could not imagine her mother being tortured by her father because she had brought home a fatherless baby to be taken care of.

Several times she thought about Jackson and wished that fate had not been so cruel to them. One day when her daughter was about five months old and she was smiling sweetly, Joanitta decided to make Jackson aware that he was a father to a lovely bouncing baby girl. She opened the window and looked at the bright shining moon. It had a magical feel and inevitably she remembered another moonlit night some one and a half years ago. A night which had greatly changed her life.

Softly and tenderly, she sang Don Williams' song:

There's a yellow moon
Shining in the starry sky
Oh, I wonder if you're watching it, too
There's a yellow moon
Shining in the starry sky
Wherever you are it's watching over you
Oh shine on shine on
Yellow moon.

She sung as if she was singing to Jackson. When she finished the song, she gently shut the bedroom window and, in the quiet of her room, she wrote:

Darling J,
It has been more than a year since we were last in touch and the times have been really rough with me. That lovely night under the moonlight, you made me conceive your baby, a lovely bouncing

baby, whom I have named Jackie. She is right now sleeping peacefully next to me. I'm sorry I have never had any time to write and inform you of what had happened, for as soon as the school authorities found out at school, they took me back home. They did not even give me time to go back to the dormitory to pack my things. The matron saw to that. I will never forget the headmistress. She was so caring and sympathetic and had even promised to let me go back to school after delivery.

But my father! One would have thought that all the vengeful spirits of his forefathers had possessed him. He tried to extract from me the identity of the father of my child . And that was when I knew that I had to keep you in the dark from knowing what had happened, for he was swearing to rip you open if he ever landed on you — rather the father of the child. That night, my mother smuggled me out to her distant cousin's home where I have stayed since.

Here I have learnt some few lessons. I had our lovely baby through a lot of pain. To be honest I thought I was going to die but Fate has His ways. I survived but with several tears that took two months to heal. The baby was very big and my bones were not well formed yet. And the labour pains. Jackson, those excruciatingly indescribable pains were just too much to bear. I wished you were around to hold my hand and to keep rubbing my back gently, soothing away the pain.

But I dared not tell anybody the pain I was going through. How dare I when everybody had been reminding me that I asked for it. So, I bit my lower lip and consoled myself by thinking of you. When the final contraction came, I pushed with all the might as Jackie tore her way into the world.

I am a living example of how teen-age pregnancy causes interruption in education, puts the health of both the mother and the baby at risk, and adds to the economic burdens of the extended family. I now know that a woman is not physically ready to begin bearing children until she is about eighteen years of age. Babies born to women younger than eighteen are more likely to be born too early and to weigh too little at birth. Such babies are much more likely to die in the first year of life. The risk to the mother's own health is also greater.

Sweetheart, the girl is your photocopy. And when I see her sweet smiling face, I console myself that all was not in vain. Her sweet smiles, together with that first letter you wrote me, keep the fire in me burning — that low burning fire you first lit in me on that moonlit night. To borrow Judy Butcher's words:

*I'm dreaming of a little island
Just big enough for two
Making up for all we've been missing
In this land I'm dreaming of.*

It has reached a point where I must leave my aunt's home. Sweetheart, everything that goes wrong in this house is blamed on me and the child. I am not sure where I am going to. If you ever get this letter, do not attempt to write back because I have no permanent address. But I am going to the big city in the hope that I can start life afresh.
All the best, darling.
Your ever loving love,
J

That night she packed her few belongings. And as the first cocks were about to crow their good morning to a new day, she left her aunt's home to start life afresh in the city.

A sacrifice for Maayi

Ayeta Anne Wangusa

She was twelve yeas old but had been in primary four for four years. This was not a strange occurrence since all the girls in her class seemed to be much older than the class they were in.

In Bunambutye village, there was only one primary school which the school children avoided happily. Perhaps this was because the school was located under the big tree next to Bunambutye Church of Uganda. The two teachers who were attached to this Harambee school chose to teach when there was a shade. During the rainy season, they never reported to the school at all. And when the dry season came, the kids were home with running noses. This explains why children like Maliza stagnated in one class for so long.

Maliza's parents were poor peasants . She had two brothers who were older than her. The only sister she had joined the next world at the tender age of six when malaria struck her down.

Like the average Gisu peasant family, one would expect a cow or two in the kraal outside their mud and wattle hut. This was not the case in Mzee Wambwa's household because the Karamojong cattle rustlers had taken away the five cows he had managed to gather over the years.

Left almost penniless, Mzee Wambwa became irritable when Maliza one day returned from school with a letter indicating that she would not be allowed in school the next term because she had not paid school fees for the last two terms.

"What! I thought I gave you money for your school fees?" thundered Mzee Wambwa.

"You ...you only paid half of the fees of the last term of last year," stammered Maliza.

"Well, as you can see....my cows are gone. Where do you expect me to get your fees from? You have to stay home and help your mother with the housework," he said with a resigned expression.

Maayi Khaukha, Maliza's mother, who was splitting firewood near the kitchen came in to rescue her daughter.

"Paapa, you can't give up so easily. We still have our garden to look to. Maliza can still go to school," she appealed to Maliza's father.

"Why should she go to school when we can barely afford it! I still have a debt with the school ...." he roared.

"The maize in the garden is enough to pay for the school fees..."

"Woman, are you crazy? That maize is meant for the granary and not to pay school fees. When the clouds dry up, what happens to us? Do you want us to become beggars in our own village? There will be no more talk about school, understand?" Mzee Wambwa commanded as he stormed away using the path that went up the hill into the green thicket.

Maliza, who had witnessed everything, could not contain herself. She let her tears roll down her face in silence. She walked to her mother's kitchen and began wrapping the *matooke* in the banana leaves. She worked vigorously with her hands, tucking the last leaf around the food and was just in time to stop her mucus from dropping onto it. She blew her nose with the bottom end of her dress then lifted the soot stained sauce pan onto the tripodfire stones.

She was angry that all the keen interest she had in education had now come to naught. She raised her eyes and looked at Mukholi's house just a stone's throw from her father's house. She saw Mukholi's wife rocking her baby to sleep. Her heart misseda beat. It had not occurred to her that if she was not going to school, then there would be no excuse for her to reject any suitor's hand in marriage.

Maliza's lip trembled at the thought that her dream to become a school teacher like Muckha Wanzira was shattered. Tears came out in hot spasms and she could not control her burning emotions. She began crying loudly.

Maayi Khaukha looked down at her daughter and said, "Stop mourning, Maliza. I am not yet dead," she shouted. "School is not everything in the world!"

She would have slapped her hard had she not seen her cousin Naume from the city walking up the path that led to their homestead. Maayi Khaukha had not seen her in a long time .She dropped the axe and run to welcome her.

"*Khwakhwi nyayile* (We are happy to see you)!" she exclaimed as they embraced. Maliza's mother offered to carry the bag Naume was carrying to the house. Maliza had tried to dry her face but could not disguise the sunken look.

"What is it, my dear?" aunt Naume asked as Maliza knelt down to greet her .

"Your daughter is sulking because we can no longer afford to send her to school," said Maliza's mother.

"Don't cry, my girl, you never know ...life may prove to be better for you outside school !"

"It can't be. I wanted to become a school teacher !" Maliza said with a shaky voice.

"Really? Well, I think there are better things than becoming a teacher in the city," her aunt said.

"Is that so? Then why don't I come with you ..." Maliza asked with excitement.

"Your parents must agree over this," she said not wanting to commit herself.

"It's alright with me," Maliza's mother said hurriedly, praying that her cousin took her daughter to the city because she knew that was the only way Maliza would get a better future than the life she was leading.

That night after supper, Mzee Wambwa happily agreed that Maliza goes with his sister-in-law. Naume had butterflies in her stomach because she could not let her cousin know that the reason for her visit to Bunabutye was to pick up a house maid.

Maliza, on her part, was very happy to leave her small village. But her excitement was drowned with fear because this was her first time she was going to travel in a car. She threw up in the taxi and the passengers cursed about the stale bean odour that filled the air.

In the city, she was overwhelmed by the fast moving life style but more, she was shocked when instead of going to school, her aunt sent her to the kitchen. Maliza scrubbed saucepans and prepared all the meals for her aunt's household. In short, she made the house look pleasant for her aunt's husband to live in. She prayed daily, hoping that she would soon be given a chance to go to school. But all this was wishful thinking. The months flew by and soon it was one year after her arrival in the city. She decided to confront her aunt.

"When will I go to school?" she asked. Her aunt paused before answering her.

"Young girl, you are thirteen. Schools in the city cannot admit a girl as big as you to P4. Don't worry, next year you will go to a tailoring school."

"Tailoring school!" Maliza exclaimed. She did not have much time to brood over how her sly aunt had coaxed her parents into letting her come to the city. Maliza's cousin, Mareku, who had visited them had reported to Mzee Wambwa that Maliza was not in school but was working in Naume's kitchen.

Mareku did not know that he had driven the last nail in Maliza's coffin. Mzee Wambwa sent his son, Mukholi, to fetch Maliza. Maliza was so thrilled to see her brother. They embraced heartily before he told his aunt that his father demanded the return of Maliza to his household.

Maliza was so excited all through the journey back home. She tried to talk to her brother but discovered that he was not warm towards her. 'Well, they had fought a lot when they were young, but did he have to hold this against her for this long?' she wondered. She decided to keep quiet altogether. When she reached her father's homestead, her first impulse was to run to the smoke filled kitchen where she expected to meet her mother. She embraced her and was surprised to see her crying.

"What's wrong, Maayi?" she asked.

"Have you not seen your father?" she asked with a trembling voice.

"No. What's wrong?"

Her mother was silent. Maliza rushed to her father's house. He had some guests so she withdrew but her father motioned her to enter. She made the formal greeting and as she was about to leave, her father addressed her, "You have been having a hard time with your aunt. It's time that you became a happy woman."

"What do you mean, father?" she asked a bit anxiously. She was certainly curious to know.

"These young men that you see are from your future husband's home. They have come to ask for your hand in marriage."

"What! But I do not even know the man. I will not get married to him."

"Don't raise your voice in front of me, child!" he commanded.

Maliza was at a loss. Could this be her life. Her mouth was agape. How could her life be a rotation of misfortune. She rushed to her mother's kitchen.

"Maayi, I will not get married to that man," she cried.

"You will, my child. There is no way out."

"I will escape and go to Kenya," Maliza threatened

"You will do no such thing. If you run away I am finished. I did not want to tell you this but you have forced me to speak," she said breathlessly before swallowing saliva."Your bride price is needed ...Your father married me ...I mean, we have been living together all these years ... but he has never paid my bride price.

"Oh my God, Maayi!"

"Don't you see? My parents are demanding that if your father does not pay the bride price, I'll have to go back to their home." Maliza's mother held her daughter's arm tightly and said, "This is the reason why you should get married. You will not let your mother bow her head in shame. I am not a child to go back and live with my parents. I am your mother. Please do this just for me." Maliza was at loss for words. She could not let down her mother even if she dreaded the whole idea of marrying a man she had not set her eyes on.

She walked to her father's house, knelt down before him and said,

"I understand everything now. You can receive the cows."

Santus

Dominic Dipio

There was no doubt that Santus was handsome. One needed only a cursory look to confirm it. It was, however, difficult to tell from his casual appearance if Santus was aware of his handsomeness. One thing stood out clear: no vanity showed about him.

Tall, athletic and given to easy volubility, Santus always wore a complacent face, with a charm that could be quite disturbing. He had an oval face which looked like a well-chiselled work of art. His smooth and hairless face made him look much younger than his age. One could almost feel he had no cares. When he smiled, he revealed a perfectly well set of teeth which were as strong and determined as a cob of maize grown on humus soil. The dimple, which showed on his right cheek whenever he smiled or talked excitedly, added to the touch of the sublime about him. He dressed in silent self-effacing colours of light blue and gray shades as if not to draw attention to himself. But even if he dressed in rugs, Santus would still be noticed for his exquisite bearing. To some of his friends in the literature class, he looked just like the Bachea of Euripides.

'But how could this be? A young man of his age and looks, in his first year in the University, in normal circumstances, would be restlessly chasing girls or being chased by them.' This was the unholy thought in the minds of his acquaintances, especially the females.

In Santus was combined the rare gifts of youthfulness, handsomeness and piety. He was more than a devoted church-goer. He praised the Lord in the morning, at noon time and again when the sun went down. These qualities made him even more attractive and charming, if without his knowledge. To many of the girls who liked making lewd jokes at him, he was the kind of person they would like to control or to have him control them. Once married to such a guy, what more could a lass need?

Before he joined Makerere University, Santus had some misgivings about the University community. He had heard many unethical stories about the place, especially about its moral life. He was therefore thrilled to find a strong Christian community in place. He saw in this the fulfilment of his hopes to become a priest. During the orientation week, he acquainted himself with the routine pattern of campus life. He was particularly interested in the daily mass programme. He would attend mass and read the Word of God daily in order to keep to the path of righteousness and not lose his vocation to the priesthood.

It was, however, clear that some brazen girls in his class were determined to give him no rest. During the lectures, a number of girls vied to sit next to him. Santus did not have to go through the process of struggling for chairs. The interested girls always booked chairs for him next to themselves. Those beckoning eyes from the girls always disconcerted him. To avoid further embarrassments, he would duck into the nearest chair next to him, and pretend not to notice those many pairs of piercing eyes almost stripping him naked. The lucky girl, feeling like a victor on a battle front, would make the most of this opportunity. She would move closer to him to check for spellings. She would at times get deliberately lost in the notes-taking process so that she could borrow his notes. In all these trials, Santus acted as the perfect gentleman. He did not appear to take advantage of any of those glaring gestures.

By his third week at the University, Santus had identified a few friends to associate with. Among them was this lady, Matilda, a secretary in the Faculty of Law who was in the same choir and prayer group with him. Single, responsible, kind and warm hearted, Matilda became for Santus a symbol of motherhood, an abode in whom he could find shelter from this mundane environment of the University. He constantly referred to her as "mum" and Matilda, single and childless, bathed in the warmth of this title. At thirty, her hopes of marriage were getting dimmer and dimmer. So she decided to take every opportunity of experiencing motherhood through nursing spiritual sons and daughters to the Lord. She belonged to that category of people who took people at their face value. She always found it strenuous to think of what lay behind the veil. Being an honest lady herself, she never doubted anyone else. This was how she dealt with her nieces and nephews who lived with her.

Although very busy with secretarial work, she generously gave Santus her time whenever he came to confide in her, sharing those intimate fears and desires of his heart. When it came to material assistance, her purse was open. What material good was hers was her son's as well.

Because he was sincere, Matilda responded to him whole-heartedly. She swore Santus was a good boy and she would do everything to protect him from getting contaminated. She would protect him from those girls she caught throwing eyes at him. Yes, she was ready to employ all her resources to guide him spiritually. She would introduce him to her friends in case she ran short of spiritual advice to give him. He was not just good, he was also handsome: that was a serious issue.

The first time they shared heart to heart, Santus came to her mum's flat at around 8:30 pm. It was a weekday. Usually on weekdays, it was not Matilda's habit to entertain visitors because the heavy work in the office left her crushed. She would rather spend the evening conserving her energy by going to bed at 9:00 pm, immediately after her night prayers. But she could bend her regular routine for this good boy's sake.

When she opened the door and found her spiritual son standing behind it, she quickly brushed aside the impulsive frown on her face, replacing it with a cushioned welcome. She knew whatever brought him must be very serious. After the usual civilities, Santus started to talk in his cool, and charming manner. It was not easy for him get it out of his chest. This intensified Matilda's anxiety. What could have happened? Did some amazon dare to molest him? Although he looked cool and reserved, one could almost see that he was using super-human effort to suppress something, something turbulent, something wanting to burst to the surface. But this something, whatever it was, was very elusive to the perception of the uninitiated. Matilda, keen as she was, could not perceive it.

Then he said sweetly, "Mum, I don't really want to disturb you, but then you are the only person I feel free to express myself to."

Matilda was enchanted and unnerved by the charm of his politeness and the knowledge that she was needed. She quickly put in,

"No, no, I am here for you. What is the use of our sisterhood and brotherhood in Christ if not to help each other?"

"What I am telling you has to do with a certain girl in my Religious Studies' class who has been pursuing me for the last week like wild fury. I really don't know what else to tell her. I told her clearly that I would like to become a priest, but she has refused to leave me alone. In fact from the time she learned that I would like to go to the seminary, she has become even more aggressive in her advances. Right now, I left her lying on my bed. I don't know what else to do."

Poor Santus. Matilda's motherly heart warmed up and leapt towards the innocent boy. How he trusted her! She would not let him down. Yes, she would give him accommodation in her sitting room. That evil girl would wait for him in vain and eventually go. But what about after that? How could she protect this good boy from such shameless campus girls? In the morning during breakfast, she told him the best way to preserve and safeguard his integrity was to join one of the many Christian associations on campus. She told him her own experience, how becoming saved and keeping in company with good friends protected her from falling into hot water all the time she was at school. Of all the options put before him, Santus chose the Charismatic prayer group. He said that would satisfy him better because he had a deep desire for prayer and to be in constant communion with the Lord. Matilda could not be happier for that choice.

In the prayer group, it did not take long for Santus to be noticed by all the members as a genuine man of prayer. The Lord was kind to him with his gifts too. He quickly received the gifts of preaching, service, selfless and disinterested love for the needy; and above all, he was endowed with the gift of speaking in tongues which made him a powerful intercessor for others. Many people flocked to him with intentions and many claimed that whenever he prayed for them, they received the favours they asked of the Lord. And it was a wonder to watch him at prayer: the countenance of his face became mellower, his attention and concentration was indestructible, his clenched fist and closed eyes indicated that he was in a trance, that he had entered a realm of deep experience. How could any God be unawakened by such concentration?

Matilda could not be happier for this wonderful son the Lord had given her. Clearly, he was making bigger spiritual strides than herself. But she was not jealous because Santus was her son. In his great humility he still continued to come to Matilda for those deep spiritual sharings for which the latter at times felt inadequate. How could he continue to come to her when she felt so much of a spiritual dwarf before him? On one such occasion, when Santus was telling her about his ecstasy in prayer, how he felt outside of himself and saw the Lord floating on thick white clouds saying to him, "My son, there is one thing I desire of you. I want you to be my priest, who will offer me worthy sacrifices in atonement for the many sins committed against my holy name," she almost told him that she was a sinner, not worthy to be confided in. She almost wanted to make her confessions to this young man who saw visions of the Lord instead of going to the priest who boasted of no such visions. She wanted to tell him about the quarrel she had had with her colleague in the office, how she was at times selfish and flared into anger. Moreover, after such experiences of intimacy with the Lord, Matilda had the impression that Santus' forehead shone like that of Jesus during the transfiguration.

All this time, Santus was becoming all the more attractive, because his holiness was perfectly matched with his handsomeness and this added to his charm. He almost became a member of Matilda's family. His presence satisfied her flair for perfectionism.

One of Matilda's nieces, called Rosette, a pretty little thing lived with her during holidays. Rosette had just completed her 'A' level exams and was waiting to join the university or a tertiary institution. Of all the girls Matilda had tried to educate, Rosette was the only one who had reached that far in studies. Matilda was ready to sacrifice everything to see to it that this girl at least reached university. She treated her delicately as the apple of her eye and was rewarded because Rosette was the type of girl who did not need to be told what to do. She was inwardly motivated to do the right thing. She quietly suffered the humiliations of her sisters who had to drop out of school because of pregnancy. She promised to her heart that she would not betray her aunt. Matilda often told her to learn from Santus' seriousness of mind. Let her be an example of one pretty girl who is also virtuous.

But this holiday, Matilda noticed something not quite in keeping with Rosette's usual self. This girl who had been so hardworking and grateful was becoming lazy and rude. Well, probably, she was feeling too big to be disturbed with domestic chores. What could be the problem? Was she pregnant? No! That could not be. Rosette was not that kind of girl, although you ccould never tell how she had behaved in school. "Lucky for Santus who had already gone to the seminary to pursue his call to follow the Lord more intimately. He will never be bothered by this kind of worries," thought Matilda.

As weeks passed by, the signs of Rosette's pregnancy were becoming more obvious. On the evening when Matilda decided to confront that angel of a girl, she was surprisingly visited by a young woman in the company of a five year old boy child. This made her postpone her interview with Rosette.

The young woman told Matilda that she had come on a very serious business. She introduced herself as the mother of Santus' love child. She presented the child to Matilda. The young woman, who called herself Rita, continued, "I have come to you because I heard that you have been very close to Santus, and that it was due to your recommendation that he has been accepted in the seminary. All I am asking is, has he explained to you how his son is going to be brought up when he is studying to become a priest?"

Matilda was besides herself with anger, shock, self-reproach and some strange feelings for which she had no name. Was the woman mad? What was she talking about? How could she drag Santus, her son into this? She was about to throw the woman out of her house as a black mailer when Rosette, who had been listening to their conversation from her room, joined them in the sitting room. In a clear and unperturbed voice, she said, "Rita is right, Santus told me about her and the child."

This interjection from Rosette threw Matilda into further confusion. Had they all conspired to torment her? What wrong had she done to any of them? Was that her reward? When the whole situation began to make sense to her, she cried out fiercely: "No! No! It can't be. It is not fair!" Then Rosette's voice floated out once again, "I am also carrying his love child." This did not make any impression on Matilda. What she had to deal with was already too much for her. After some hours of recovery, Matilda was determined to summon the rogue of a saint to come to answer to these charges. How could he fool her so? After that she would write to the seminary authority withdrawing her recommendation of him, and even advise them to send him away from the seminary.

Three weeks elapsed before Santus responded to Matilda's urgent call. During this time, Matilda's rage had cooled down. She had promised to blast the boy into splinters and to dissociate herself with him completely. But when Santus arrived, she found herself unable to do half of what she had sworn to do. The boy was still wearing that radiant holy face. When she spoke to him, it was not in anger, but in sympathy with this boy who already looked a repentant sinner. She simply said, "I know about everything. I don't want to go through it. It is too painful. Rita and the child have been here."

Santus denied nothing. He admitted all his sins. How he had lied to Matilda. How his conduct with women in all these years had been sinful. But above all, how he still felt called to the priesthood to lead sinners back to God. He was sorry for having used all those women but he just could not live with them because his love for the priesthood was stronger than the love for all the women put together. And he finally asked Matilda, if she would still take him back as her son.

The last one to know

Violet Barungi

House burns down: two believed killed

A house in Bukoto belonging to Mr. John Agaba was yesterday gutted down by fire. Two people were believed killed and property worth millions destroyed. The cause of the fire has not yet been established. The police is still investigating..

I looked at the date again before I threw the yellowed old newspaper down. It was a year old but I kept it locked away and occasionally, when I was in a morbid mood, got it out and glanced at the article to keep the tragedy fresh in my mind.

'The wife is always the last one to know' is a hackneyed phrase people are always bandying around in cases of marital deceptions in which the woman is almost always the victim. But I never imagined I would ever hear it whispered behind my back. Why does one always think that bad things happen to others and not to oneself, I wondered. But in my case, I had every reason to be complacent. I had a good husband and a good marriage. The worst my detractors could say about me, and actually did say, was that I had bewitched my husband.

"I don't believe in witchcraft," I told my friend Sheila when one day she repeated the rumours about me. "But I believe in love and mutual trust and respect," I added smugly.

"And of course John knows which side his bread's buttered," Sheila remarked with a touch of malice. She was alluding to the fact that I was the bread-winner in the family. I earned more from my small business than John did from his office job as an accountant. So I was the solvent one in the family and the provider of all the comforts we enjoyed.

But it had not always been like that. When I first married John, I was an inexperienced young girl without any training or skill of any sort.

I had gone straight from school to the altar, so to speak. For the first four years, I stayed at home having babies and learning how to become an efficient housekeeper. Of course I had domestic help, in fact many in succession and learnt a few useful tricks from some of them about home management. But they rarely stayed, leaving me high and dry. Fortunately, John was not an exacting husband. He was kind and patient and the few squabbles we had were mostly about money.

Before our marriage and immediately after, John had spent lavishly on me, giving me the impression that his bank account was an exhaustless mine, a common trend among men, especially older men who want to impress women. I am not saying that I regarded John as an old man although there was a disparity of twelve years between our ages. He was thirty and I was eighteen when we got married. But because he was not overbearing or patronising, and because we loved each other so much, the age difference seemed negligible.

But his attitude towards money soon changed. Instead of the sweet, generous spender, I had a stingy and tough disciplinarian on my hands. He demanded that I account for every nickel I spent which made my life impossible. It got so bad that I started to long for money of my own which I could spend any way I liked. I was tired of having to beg for every paltry sum with which I was expected to do miracles.

As if things were not bad enough, John was implicated in an embezzling case by his firm and suspended on half-pay while investigations were going on. This was the last straw for me. We lived in a neighbourhood where appearances mattered more than anything else. How could I hold my head up with a scandal like that! More over, how were we going to manage without his full monthly income? I shuddered at the thought of the things I would be forced to do in order to make ends meet. It also soon became apparent that we could not afford to go on paying the rent on the house, and to my relief, we moved to a less ostentatious area where we were not known.

But as I scraped and scrimped on John's meagre savings while waiting for the case to be brought to trial in court, the thought of making my own money changed from being a dream to being an obsession. I thought about it day and night but I had nobody to advise me. Although John never stopped to insist on his innocence, claiming he had been framed, it did not stop him from worrying about the outcome. He withdrew into himself completely and only came out to ram down my throat the need to save every penny.

I searched for a way out without success. John's case was eventually dismissed for lack of evidence but his company dismissed him all the same with two months' salary in lieu of notice. It was like the end of the rope.

"I'll get another job, don't worry," he comforted me. But his optimism soon turned to despondency as his applications were rejected, one after another. His qualifications, his sixteen years of experience all gone down the drain.

In the other estate where we had been living before we came down in the world, I had made one good friend called Janice. She was married to a business tycoon with fleets of mini-buses and other lucrative enterprises. Janice had appeared genuinely fond of me and after we moved away, I tried to keep in touch. When this last blow befell us, I ran to her with the idea of appealing to her to get her husband to employ John. But instead she offered me a job in her boutique shop. I accepted her offer gratefully. This was the chance I had been looking for, the golden gate to the EL Dorado of my dreams. More and more women were venturing into the business world and making a tremendous success of it. So what could possibly stop me once started? I felt excited and confident that things were about to change for the better in the Agaba family. However, there were two snags to get out of the way first. One was the need to convince John of the expedience of the move. He had the typical male attitude towards working women. He did not trust them. But the fact that he was still out of work persuaded him to reluctantly give his consent.

The second one, and by far the more tricky of the two, was the question of domestic help, a luxury I had long dispensed with. With three infants at home, it was absolutely necessary to find somebody mature and reliable to care for them while I was at the shop during the day. Fortunately, with my mother's help, I was able to get a distant cousin whose marriage had ran aground because she was childless. But when I took my first look at her, I concluded that childlessness must have been a minor part of the story. She looked so grotesque that she could only have been married to a blind man. But I was not recruiting her for a beauty contest and I knew that children are not generally very fastidious about looks. What would John make of her though, I wondered? Until he found a job, he would be cooped up in the small house with the amazon all day long.

Luckily, he soon found employment with another company, relieving my worries. Monistera, my new helper, learned her job quickly and became quite indispensable, especially where the children were concerned. At first I could not remunerate her as she deserved. I was being paid salary myself but I showed my appreciation in other ways. I could not afford to lose her.

The shop was doing well and Janice was pleased and increased my salary. In addition, she allowed me to put in my own items and by the end of the first year as her salesgirl, half the stock in the shop was mine. I was travelling overseas to do the purchasing for the shop as Janice's health was not up to it. I took advantage of the bargain sales to build my own egg nest.

As her health continued to decline, Janice took less and less interest in the business, leaving the entire management of the *The* **Smart Set to me.** She also brought in her sister, Angela, to help me but unfortunately the latter had a distrustful nature and started poking her nose into my business, insinuating that I was cheating her sister. This prompted me to start my own business. I had enough saved to do this in a humble way to begin with.

I discussed this with John, I never took a step without seeking his advice. He understood economic business trends better than I, and I also did not want him to feel sidelined. He encouraged me in my endeavour and promised me all the help he could. His confidence in my business capability had long been vindicated. Later, with our combined incomes, we bought a plot in Bukoto and put up a house which we managed to complete within a year. My business prospered and with the profits I was making, I bought good furniture for the house and put in modern gadgets and generally made life easy and comfortable for everybody, especially my husband, whose financial burden was greatly reduced. By the time of our tenth anniversary, he was only making token contribution to the family welfare. But I did not mind this because I knew that without his support, I would not have managed to succeed in what I was doing. Most of the business women I knew were always lamenting their husbands' lack of support which quite often ended in their having to choose between marriage and economic independence.

I was extremely busy and mobile in those days. I worked long hours and came home dead tired most of the time. The only day I had for my family was Sunday but even that, I mostly spent it in bed recharging for the next six days. But my husband's support was half the story. The other half was the security I got knowing that I had a reliable, faithful and indefatigable friend at home as a back-up. Monistera had taken over the reins of my home and turned it into a haven. My children, now all of school going age, looked happy and well-cared for; my husband was contented and I was free to do my business without the hustle of unreliable and problematic domestic staff most other working women were faced with. I was travelling abroad on business at least four times a year and always felt at liberty to stay as long as it was necessary to get good value for my money.

Another problem which plagued most women from all walks of life was the bestial nature of men generally, which was particularly of great concern in this age of the AIDS scourge. But John was not that kind of man and I trusted him completely. When would he find the time to play fast and loose, anyway? He came straight home from office and hardly ever stirred out without me. But these occasions, when the two of us could go out together, were getting fewer as I got busier. I always got home after seven by which time I would be only fit for a bath and bed. My sister, Betty, was always urging me to get somebody to assist in the shop so that I could have more time with my family. But in my heart I knew that whatever I was doing, I was doing for the good of all of us concerned. Besides, whom could I trust with my precious goods? The only person I could count upon not to pilfer from me was Monistera but I needed her at home. I was completely dependent on her. She knew more about my children's needs and desires; my husband's tastes and idiosyncrasies than I did. She was all encompassing; she was the tops!

It never occurred to me that she might be deliberately undermining me and trying to alienate me from my family. I was smug in my role as a benefactor and accepted her total devotion unquestioningly. I had taken her out of rags and given her everything she had in the world. How could I have known that underneath the meek exterior lurked a predatory nature or that my solid husband, the only man in the world whose honour I could swear to with my dying breath, could turn out to be such a rotter!

The last one to know

Violet Barungi

Monistera had been with me for four years when she became pregnant. It would have been a time of joy for a woman who had been cast away for being barren, but it was not. Monistera was not married and nobody seemed to know who the father of her child was. Some people, like my sister, made it their pre-occupation to find out but it was not mine. As far as I was concerned, it could have been the metre-reader from UEB, the Water Board or the angel, Gabriel, I really did not give a damn. My main interest in her condition was to ensure that she could still do the job I had brought her to do, and that she did not have silly ideas like leaving us to marry the father of her child. Having ascertained, to my satisfaction, that the status quo would be upheld, I promised her all the help possible and put the matter, or tried to put the matter out of my mind. But Betty and John made such a fuss over it as to make it appear like a national disaster. Betty was a natural born busy-body; I could understand why she would not rest until she had delved out Monistera's deepest secret. But what possible interest could John have in my cousin-maid's condition? He did not only show passing interest, he actually suggested I should get rid of her, arguing that she would be of little help to me once she had a baby of her own to look after! The argument was tenable but it showed a callous side to his nature I had never suspected. But I could not think of a life without Monistera and closed my ears to their reasoning.

Monistera's baby was fantastically beautiful. Everybody who saw him said so. "He looks exactly like Junior when he was born, doesn't he?" I remarked improvidently and heard a loud in-take of breath from somebody. A minute later, John walked out of the room.

"My God," Betty exclaimed incredulously, "you really are obtuse!" Nambi, the girl I had engaged temporarily to help around until Monistera was back on her feet, went into a paroxysm of giggles. She was a cheeky girl and I did not like her very much, but even so, I was surprised when Betty raised her hand and slapped her hard on the cheek.

"What did you do that for?" I asked her angrily as Nambi ran out of the room, making two angry withdraws so far. "I don't want to have any problems with her until Monistera has recovered fully." In my mind, I saw myself forced to abandon the business and staying at home to look after the family after Nambi had withdrawn her services- no, no, I could not afford that.

"Have you had a good look at the baby, Ruth?" Betty asked me with a sidelong glance at Monistera.

"Why?" I looked at her inquiringly but something in her attitude made me turn to look at Monistera. She was sitting on her bed in the posture of somebody in deep meditation. "You're trying to tell me something, right?"

"Praise God I've got through to your thick skull at long last," Betty said ironically.

"Well, out with it. It's not like you to beat about the bush," I retorted impatiently. I had wasted enough time already for one day and I had a business trip to Hongkong to prepare for.

"I don't have anything more to add to what I've already said. But perhaps dear Monistera might," she added, her tone oozing sarcasm. "Yes, Monistera, did you say something?" she mocked as Monistera burst into tears. I am not exactly stupid and I was beginning to cotton onto her meaning. I stood perfectly still for some minutes, listening to Monistera's pathetic weeping and thinking to myself that the last thing an ugly person should do is cry in public. Ugly? Beauty is in the eyes of the beholder or John wouldn't have ... I stopped as my mind feebly fought to keep reality at bay. Suddenly, piercing sounds from the wick-cradle offered me the much needed reprieve. I bent down and picked up the swathed bundle and crooned it in my arms. When it had quietened down, I took a few seconds to study it before I handed it to its mother who was watching me with a frightened expression.   "He wants to feed," I said quietly. At that point, Betty walked out of the room, bristling with impatience and I followed more pensively.

"It's time to wake up, Ruth," she said as soon as we were out of the room.

"It's not true, is it? John could not have done that to me, not with a person like Monistera!" I shook my head dazedly as I collapsed on the bed.

"I tried to warn you, Ruth, but you would not listen," Betty responded in her usual insensitive way. She came and sat beside me saying, "You cannot go on denying the truth, Ruth, with concrete evidence like that before you. You yourself remarked on the resemblance between Junior and Monistera's baby."

"Don't you dare compare my child to th..at..t creature,"I screamed at her. "Don't you ever dare say that again."

"I'm sorry, Ruth, I was only trying....."

"Don't say anything more, you've said enough already," I stormed, turning my anger against her. I got up and went to the dresser where John's framed picture seemed to be giving me a quizzical look. I picked it up and studied it silently, gazing into the warm, direct eyes set in a deep crater. Eyes that had instantly bowled me over the first time we met and had kept me enthralled ever since. What could such eyes see in a lump of flesh like Monistera? Had I changed so much to warrant his turning to a person like that? I looked critically at myself in the mirror: I had always tended to plumpness and had recently gained extra weight but I was still young at twenty eight and retained most of my good looks. I could understand if he had turned to somebody like Betty. She and I shared the same patrician features of our ancestors but she was two years younger than I and a lot slimmer. "Do you think I've changed so much, Betty, from what I looked like when he married me?" I appealed to her.

"Don't be an idiot, Ruth, you're still a head-turner," she told me kindly. I did not know whether to believe her or not in view of her ever constant reminders to watch my cholesterol in-take. I touched the folds of my overlapping stomach with disgust. "Anyway, to men all cats are black in the night."

"Am I supposed to be comforted by that?" I snorted. "I thought John was different from other men. And what's more, I can't understand why he chose Monistera. He could have had his pick of all the young and beautiful women in town, it wouldn't have hurt so much, but Monistera! I feel so humiliated; I'll never be able to hold my head up again, oh, oh!"

"Well, I'll tell you what I think. Proximity and availability play a big part in affairs like this. John's not a bad man really, that's why he had to make do with what was available."

"Explain yourself," I said dangerously. "Are you insinuating that I've been neglecting him?"

She didn't answer but I could see it on her face that she thought exactly that. And she was right. I was always too tired to play my role as a wife properly.

"The saddest thing is that you could have prevented all this if you had heeded my advice," Betty, who never knew when to leave well alone, went on. "You surely cannot convince me that you did not sense anything when everybody else around you did. You couldn't have been all that blind."

Not blind but complacent, pleased with my lot. There were incidents which could have opened my eyes to what was going on if I had been alert. In particular I remembered how I would wake up at night to find John's side of the bed empty. But I always assumed he was in the bathroom. I had no reason to suspect anything else. Besides, I used to take sleeping tablets most of the time to help me relax and as a result tended to confuse reality with illusion. There were other little things, which when considered within the context of what had taken place, assumed tremendous significance. As Betty correctly put it, I had eyes but I was unwilling to use them.

"These things happen, Ruth."

"What do you mean by that?" I exploded. "Are you trying to tell me that I should take it lying down? Do you know how much I have sacrificed for John, beginning with leaving school prematurely to marry him when I could have had a good education like you and got a good job instead of working my fingers to the bone to keep the family comfortable?"

"Be fair, Ruth, it was your choice," Betty pointed out.

"I was pregnant, what other choice did I have? Anyway, whose side are you on?"

"Your side of course but....."

"Don't you 'but' me! Look at all these things in the house, the house itself, whose money do you think made it possible? Mine, I tell you, mine, do you hear? John's share does not even add up to one tenth. And yet he has the.... the.... I don't know what to call it...to forget all this!"

"Take it easy..."

"I'll not take it easy," I snapped. "I've made that monster what she is; I've never denied John anything. If my physical attraction has waned, what about my economic value? I made him what he is now, got him out of the slum and helped him build this house he can be proud of, and how does he repay me? By sleeping with my house girl and making me an object of ridicule! I'm not going to let him get away with it, I tell you: I am not. Where's he hiding anyway?"

"I think he has gone," Betty said watching me worriedly. "I heard

The last one to know

Violet Barungi

the car start while we were still in Monistera's room.... where are you going?" she added as I reached for my shoes.

"I'm going to find him and kill him," I told her between clenched teeth.

"Wait, don't be hasty, Ruth. You'll not achieve anything except make a spectacle of yourself," she cautioned.

"If you did not want me to make a spectacle of myself, why did you tell me?" I challenged. "Besides, I couldn't make myself more of a spectacle than I am already."

"You need time to think about it.... plan something more effective than a public confrontation."

"You know something, Betty? You're full of shit," I told her venomously but all the same she prevailed upon me to abandon my chase and forced me to take a sedative.

I did not wake up until the next morning, feeling groggy and depressed. The anger was still there although the urge to strike out was somehow reduced. I conceded that I needed time to think everything out through before I made any major decision. But one point I was quite clear about, I was not going to allow the two of them to go on as if nothing had happened. They had ruined my life, destroyed my faith in my fellow humans completely: I had to find a way of paying them back in kind.

The atmosphere in the house in the next few days was so tense that even the children felt it. John and I did not talk to each other except when absolutely unavoidable. I went about fuming while he watched and waited for the storm to break. Monistera wisely kept to her room but the sound of her baby's cries drove spikes through my head. But when I was about ready to burst, fate stepped in and took matters out of my hands with her usual disregard for consequences.

I was in the shop a few days later when I was called to the phone. "Your house is on fire," an excited neighbour announced.

"My house on fire?" I repeated dazedly but my concerned friend had not waited to fill me in with the details. I shook myself out of the stupor and the next minute saw me sprinting across the street in search of a taxi.

In Bukoto, on the spot where our house had stood was now an inferno of falling beams and collapsing walls. A crowd of people made a human cordon around the place that was almost impenetrable. My heart in my mouth, I forced my way through until I stood perilously within feet of the smouldering fire the fire-engine was ineffectively trying to put out. All sorts of rumours were flying around me: four people were reported killed in the house, others three.... "....the house girl and her baby, and the husband who was poaching on her, you know. So the wife must have decided to kill off the lot..." courtesy of Nambi, that, I supposed. The latter figure could, in my estimation, be accurate although the identities of the victims could be mixed up for John and I had left together in the car in the morning. Later I was told by the police that only two people were feared dead, an adult and an infant.

They interviewed me and John later. The cause of the fire was still a mystery. There were no combustible substances in the house, I assured them, except a small container of paraffin. They told us that the girl, Nambi, had already been interviewed but could not throw light on the matter either. According to her statement, she had not been anywhere near the place. She had gone to the market and when she came back the house was already ablaze.

What could have caused the fire, I kept wondering. I considered Nambi briefly who had come to us without references but what reason would she have for so heinous an act? Besides, I did not think she was ingenious enough to execute a full-proof plan. If she were responsible, it could only be by accident, which would explain her keeping out of my sight.

Throughout the interview with the police, I noticed that John kept giving me speculative glances and when it was confirmed that the bodies burnt beyond recognition corresponded to those of Monistera and her baby, he actually gaped as if I were a witch who had willed the tragedy. Later, I learnt that he indeed suspected me of the horrendous act. But granted that I was that evil, how could I have destroyed the house I had contributed the greater share to build and which contained all the fruits of my years of hard work? For that matter, he could have done it to extricate himself from an awkward position. But immediately I thought of this, I dismissed it as untenable. John was anything but practical or ruthless. He was the type who always waited for problems to solve themselves or left it to others to do it for him.

***

It was now a year since we had lost our house and all our property. I had put the children in boarding schools when John and I moved to a small house where we lived together like strangers, haunted by the ghosts of Monistera and her baby. Our marriage was over but what I could not understand was why he did not leave me. Every evening I came back from my small grocery shop nearby, I expected to find him gone but he was always there, waiting for me.

I reached for the newspaper and folded it carefully before putting it back in the small drawer where I kept it locked away. I wished I could lock away all the memories of the past year with it, but alas, they were always there, day and night.

On my way to the kitchen, I happened to glance through the window overlooking the front of the house and saw two women heading towards the house. As they drew closer, I recognised Nambi but the other woman was a complete stranger to me.

"Well," I said loudly, "guess who has decided to appear after a year. Nambi herself. If she has come to claim her wages or her property destroyed in the fire, she has a surprise in store for her." John raised his eyes from the book he was reading questioningly. He had long lost the art of speech.

I received Nambi and her companion coolly. The former looked sullen as if she had been dragged there against her will. The older woman, on the other hand, was all smiles. She introduced herself as Nambi's mother. Then with a fanatical glow, she launched into a long testimony about her life before and after she became born-again. I congratulated her and urged her to come to the point. It later transpired that her daughter had come to let us know that she had been withholding vital evidence in connection with the fire.

"What evidence?" John and I exclaimed at the same time.

"You must excuse my daughter, she did not know at the time how important it was. That's why she said nothing to the police."

"What didn't she know?" I asked sharply.

"About the can of petrol."

"Why don't you let Nambi tell it in her own words," John suggested gently as I was about to bark another question. Nambi looked at him gratefully.

"What you're saying, Nambi, is that before you went to the market, Monistera asked you to buy her a can of petrol at the petrol station?"

"Yes," Nambi said, tears running down her cheeks. "She told me she had a toothache, how could I have known that she wanted to burn the house with herself and the baby in it?"

"You couldn't," John soothed her. "Don't worry about it; you've done the right thing to come to us now with the information and we are grateful," he assured her. I had a few questions and vituperations I wanted to fling at her like how her stupidity had cost me a year of my marriage but before I could open my mouth, John had given them transport money back and was speeding them on their way. They left amidst choruses of 'Praise God'.

So what now, I thought stealing a glance at John's closed face. Surely he was not going to lay Monistera's suicide at my door! I waited for his comments but all he said was, "I'm sorry, Ruth." Sorry? Was that enough for the mental torment, the feeling of loss and emptiness inside me? Did I still want revenge against him? But as I searched my mind, I knew that I could not have thought of a more effective way to torture him than the year he had spent at my side not knowing whether I was a murderer or not, or the knowledge that Monistera had committed suicide and he was responsible for it.

"It doesn't matter now," I replied. This was of course far from a perfect reconciliation but it was a beginning; a sign that one day it might be possible for us to live like a family again.

Where is she?

Philo Nabweru

The bowl containing the fruit salad slipped from her hands and shattered at her feet. She swore and reached for a broom to clear the mess. Before she could execute the first stroke, a toddler came tumbling towards her. She dropped the broom quickly and held the child before giving a sharp cry of pain as a splinter of glass entered her left foot. The plump foot immediately spurted blood. She looked at her foot and whimpered. The sight of blood seemed to scare her so much that she almost dropped the baby.

The baby's hand caught a strand of her black hair and stuffed it in his mouth. She jumped as if stung by a bee and flung the infant into a chair. The baby yelped so loudly that his dad, steel in his underpants, came hurrying in.

In a thunderous voice, he demanded to know what was going on. "Can't you answer or are you deaf?" he shouted.

The baby crept under the chair and stopped crying. The woman, whose large eyes stared as though they would pop out, did not say anything; neither did she move. He reached her in three long strides and pulled her towards himself. He got hold of her long hair with both hands and shook her until her teeth chattered. He pulled it so hard you could see the veins in her face standing out. He went on screaming at her as if he were demented. The woman kept muttering something inaudible as if she were going to develop an epileptic fit.

He administered several slaps to her upturned face and released her as suddenly as he had grabbed her. She landed heavily right on top of the mess of the broken dish.

She let out a heartrending wail, calling on God and her mother alternatively. *"Ai, ai Mawe. Ai, Ruhanga wange; nyowe nkakoraki!"* (Oh, my mother, my God; whatever sin did I commit!)

If it had not been for the long gown she wore, the broken glass would have entered all over her body. Looking completely unnerved, she sat there, rocking herself as she whimpered and moaned.

After a while, she gingerly picked herself up and wobbled towards a door. She entered the bathroom and examined her bruised, beautiful face in the mirror. A torrent of tears rolled down her face unchecked. She sobbed endlessly, making one think she would never stop. She regretted having ever married that man - that Mugurusi, whom everybody had warned her against! How people had talked; and how she had ignored them all! How so much in love they had been! How completely absorbed in each other they had become that no threat had been enough to stop their inevitable union into marriage!

She now thought of and remembered those times her bridegroom had carried her to their huge bed upstairs to make love. She recollected the numerous times he had held and kissed her; the lovely times they had had at dinners, dances, parties; the countless presents he had showered on her; the dresses, shoes, broaches, watch, the list was endless.

She thought of the times they had both gone to visit his or her parents. She dag out all the memories of their three year marriage, looking for the basis of her husband's violent behaviour but could find none. The troubled woman raked her brains for any major mistakes she could have committed but in vain. For that matter, she looked for a reason to hate him but found none either. Her love was so deep, so fathomless and as endless as a spider's web.

She thought of running off with the baby but wondered where she would go! Her father, may God rest his soul, had died only a few months back; her poor mother was now so old, broken and helpless. How could she go to her with more troubles! Her only brother had wedded recently and his bride had minced no words about 'not wanting any relatives snooping around'. "Oh dear God; *Bikira Maria* (Blessed Mary), where can I go?" she repeated again and again.

After what seemed like eternity, she stopped the soul-searching and looked at her foot again. It was beginning to swell and the piece of glass seemed to have been swallowed up in the skin already! She remembered what she had once read in the newspapers that a piece of glass could find its way to the heart via the blood vessels and pierce it, killing one, just like that. Her heart pounded faster as she nervously searched for it and quickly pulled it out. A small stream of blood followed this action. She opened the tap and began to wash away the blood. Now, how could she apply the painful iodine? Who would put it on for her? Her husband had been the one to do such things for her. "But now.... now....."

Meanwhile, Mr. Mugurusi had picked up the child from under the chair and placed him on a settee. He gave him a bottle full of milk which he had found on the table in a blue bucket. He sat down watching him as he sucked away. The bottle slipped once from the infant's small hands but Mugurusi quickly put it back before the baby could start crying. He too was thinking and remembering the wonderful times he had had with his wife, Migisa Anne. He recalled her sweet smile, her lilting laugh that still pulled at his heart. He suddenly realised how much he missed it because it was so rare these days! It was what had attracted him to her in the first place. He would give anything to hear it now and always. He longed for the times they would hold each other, kissing and caressing. He still felt overwhelmed by the memory of their first love-making when he had discovered that she was still a virgin!

He felt his body tingling all over and wished he could bring himself to apologise to her. How he needed her! To hold her all night long... but no, a man was a man. He could not go to her now to beg for her love. After all, it was his right to be loved. Couldn't she see that? She had no right to hold this baby all night as though he no longer existed. He could not bear those kisses she bestowed on the angelic face of their son. He could not tolerate the love she obviously lavished on him. All that love, all of it, was his. He was not ready to share it with anyone.....not even with his first born child.... no, no, nooo!

He did not quite hate the baby. He loved him in a funny sort of way; a love-hate kind of emotion. For instance, when he saw the baby separate from Anne, he could touch and smile at him; but something seemed to tighten and then loosen inside him the moment he saw that cherubic being in his wife's arms. He could not explain it. A devil seemed to possess him and it was all he could do to control the impulse that told him to get that child out of the way. He wanted, if he could, to get that baby and fling him at the wall opposite.

"That... that would teach him taking away my wife," he muttered again and again. His eyes blazed with hatred as he looked at the baby who had fallen asleep on the settee and wore a peaceful babyish smile on his handsome face. He was a photostat copy of Mugurusi indeed!

Mugurusi had to rush from the room to prevent himself from yielding to the temptation to harm the baby. He entered the bedroom expecting to find his dear Anne there. He looked all round him and even under the bed. He checked in the closet but she was nowhere to be seen. He started a systematic search of the whole house only avoiding the room where the baby slept.

"Where could she be!" he wondered. "Oh Anne. Please forgive me! Do not leave me... I love you so! Please God... do not let her go away!" Mugurusi kept muttering under his breath as he moved from room to room. When he had gone through all the rooms, he went to the kitchen. She wasn't there either. "Good Lord, where can she have gone?"

He sat at the kitchen table, a place he usually sat watching Anne cooking. He folded his arms on the table and rested his head on them. He closed his eyes and proceeded to visualise Anne preparing dinner. The dough for chapati, chopping onions, slicing cabbage... he saw her beautiful busy hands transform the mess on the table into mouth-watering items. He conjured up her arm around his shoulders and he shivered. "Anne, oh my darling Migisa. Let us get back together now!" he whispered over and over. "My dear Innocent, Immaculate heart... my life... I can't live without you." He went on and on whispering endearments to his sweet darling Anne whom he had turned so much against.

Anne was determined to end her misery that day. The last ten months, which she had termed the 'for worse', of her marriage, had to end that day. She could not go on facing her husband whom she loved and yet could not dare go near. Perhaps he had got himself a secret lover as other men did. May be he was a Nubian as people often whispered! May be he would, one of these days, cut her up and cook her! She again thought of going to confide in her old mother. Perhaps she would give her advice. But where would she pass. Mugurusi was bound to stop her. She recalled the much-talked-of, famous witch doctor on Masaka Road, re-nowned for her potent love medicines but hurriedly dismissed the idea when she remembered what had happened to her cousin's husband. Her cousin had been given a love potion by some witch doctor which had proved fatal when she administered it to her husband.

"Hmmmh," she sighed. An appropriate way had to be found to end Mugurusi. Yes, something had to be done very soon. Yet every progress she made in her plans to cause his death kept being interrupted by her love for him. She kept making excuses to counter each accusation.

But love or not, something had to be done to avenge herself. "And it has to be tonight...TO NIGHT..." She looked into the medicine cabinet and saw all the neatly arranged containers of panadol, magnesium, chloroquine, aspirin, insecticide... should she swallow some overdose and die there in the bathroom? She could even swing herself on that metal wire they spread their underwears on to dry... At this thought, she shuddered involuntarily. No... something had to be done first about Mugurusi.... the cause of it all...that night.

Her mind so made up, she put a bandage on her swollen foot and left the bathroom. She moved purposefully to the dining room, swept away the mess from the doorway and cleared away the dishes that still contained the lunch that no one had touched. Then she returned and looked over at the settee where her handsome son lay, still peacefully asleep. How so much like her husband he looked! "Why did Mugurusi have to behave in such a beastly manner? Why indeed!" But tonight, he would learn a lesson. She, Migisa Anne, daughter of Kakyomya, would teach him...

Returning to the kitchen, she settled down to doing one of the tasks she enjoyed most. She loved cooking. It appealed to her need to create, to transform, to serve. May be she would be doing it for the last time? Who knew what she would do that night? May be she could escape? To Fort Portal where her mother's sister stayed or to her uncle who lived in Hoima? Her mind whirled round and round as her busy hands went ahead to create appetising dishes from the confusion on the table. Soon there was a salad, pudding and chapati. She sniffed appreciatively at the rice cooking. This is a field she had no doubts about. "It is not like my marriage these days," she sighed.

After putting the pudding and chapatis in the oven and the salad in the refrigerator, she scrubbed the dishes and pans mechanically, hanging them on nails provided at one side of the table for that purpose. This done, she moved away from the kitchen to check on the baby who still slumbered on. In her bedroom upstairs, she cleaned herself up, combed her hair in one of the latest hairdos and dressed up in a pink dress. As she moved downstairs, she heard her husband's quick footsteps enter the house through the side door. He called for her over and over. Her heart leaped painfully as she noiselessly slid behind a door. For a moment, the profusion of emotions that voice always roused in her screamed for her to answer but she throttled them with a will she hadn't imagined to possess. She let him pass by, rushing towards their bedroom.

"Anne... Anne... Anneeee," he yelled. "Where are you? Come on, where are you? Come out I say!"

Anne hurried to the kitchen and brought out the food onto the dining table so quickly that by the time Mugurusi came down again, she was seated at the head of the table, seemingly, in pefect control and managed to present a calm picture.

He approached her very swiftly and she winced in anticipation of the now usual lashing. He arrested her in a tight embrace, crushing her to himself. Anne struggled and kicked to free herself. Mugurusi held her like a vice and was oblivious of anything else but the ecstasy of the close contact.

She was desperate, gasping for breath, her whole body recoiling from the sudden closeness. Her hand gropped for something....it reached the bottle of after-dinner wine which she brought crushing on Mugurusi's head. Too stunned to react, Mugurusi simply stared. Anne pulled a drawer open and snatched out a bread knife. She advanced towards her dazed husband, knife poised like a butcher's panga. She moved fast... her face set and her mouth working. It looked like she was in a trance. Mugurusi stood rooted to where he was, dumbfounded; mesmerised by the demoniac light in her eyes and the terrible half-smile on her lips. She kept repeating something under her breath. It sounded like "Dododoo, doo now!"

At the moment the knife made contact with Mugurusi's body, there was a seemingly far away cry. Anne glanced in that direction and noticed her son struggling to move from where he had fallen. His mouth was bloody. In that instant, she knew what she had to do... Throwing the chair out of her way, she dashes towards the child, her hand brandishing the sharp knife. Just as she reached the child, Mugurusi woke up from the stupor and yelled for her to stop. She did not look back. She kept moving like a sleepwalker.

"We've. *iwe*... Eeeeh! Don't do it!" he shouted with all his might. Like a cat caught stealing, she jumped away from the infant.... stopped...... looked at Mugurusi and started moving away from him. The backward movement brought her against the wall. She looked at the knife and then pointed it at her breast. At that instant, Mugurusi realised how much he had wronged her as to cause her to want to die. He had to save her. How he loved her!

"Please, Anne, put away that knife. I will never, ever mistreat you again. I love you so much! Please forgive me. I have been such a fool to be jealous of our child!" As he pleaded with her, she wondered whether he really meant any of what he was saying.

She shook her head. "Good bye, my love," she whispered. She turned... stopped and looked back once.... and started running blindly out of the house.

Mugurusi chased after her, hoping and praying that he would catch up with her before she used that knife.

Hidden identity

Goretti Kyomuhendo

I was born in Wangaale, a small landing site on the shores of lake Munyonyi, in the small township of Mityana. This small village of ours could only be accessed by a creaking boat and once you entered it, you had to say your last prayers, name your heir and make all your last wishes because you could never be too sure whether you would come out of it alive or not. Stories were abound of how this same boat had ever capsized, not once, but several times, killing all aboard, and how many sacrifices had been offered before it could be put to use again.

In those days when I was growing up, mothers were the sole caretakers of homes. This meant that they would stay at home, tending to farms, rearing children and making sure that members of their families had food on their plates. The men, on the other hand, would go hunting and come back late in the evening- with or without the meat, depending on the mood of the gods that day. If the gods were in the happy mood, they would shower one with a bounty of as much as two animals, but if they were angry...

The men, on coming back, would order the young children to fetch water for them from the well for washing their blood-stained bodies, before going off to join their other fellow men in beer-drinking clubs. They would not come back until past midnight when they would demand for the roasted meat they had left the wives preparing.

I remember the story about hunting my mother told us when I was about eight years.

"Listen to this story, my children," my mother had began. "There was a woman who was both my friend and neighbour and whose husband was a hunter just like your father. In those days, the men in the hunting party, which normally comprised of all the able-bodied young men in the village, would send one of them ahead to come and inform the wives that the gods had been merciful that day. The wives would of course understand the message. So one day, one such a messenger was sent to come and tell my neighbour and friend that her husband had been killed by an elephant. This woman, however, understood it to mean that her husband had killed an elephant. She subsequently poured the green vegetables she had prepared for dinner and invited all her friends to come and share in the feasting which was bound to follow. It was so sad. The party which followed instead came to mourn the dead man!" my mother concluded.

My father was not particularly a good hunter, so the other men in the village said. They always despised him for his cowardice and scorned him for being lazy. They said that he could not even participate in the ferrying of the meat after it was cut into pieces. As a result, my father had very few friends, if any, in their hunting groups. But he always went on the defensive whenever this topic was brought up by my mother. He said that his own mother had warned him never to make friends with hunters. According to her, hunters could only be friends before the kill. After that, it was everyone for his stomach. Of course my mother never bought that, we all knew how difficult my father was and how impossible it was for him to sustain any kind of relationship. Hunting was, however, not his full time occupation and after a time, he quit it altogether.

I had long learnt that I was not my father's favorite child- in fact, his feelings for me bordered on hate. In my small mind, I suspected that it was due to something bad I had done or said to him. One day, I asked my mother why my father felt like this towards me.

"When you are a bit older, I will explain all this to you and you will understand," my mother had answered.

"Can't you tell me now, mother? I surely want to know," I insisted.

It was raining heavily that day and we were all seated in the small kitchen waiting for my father to come back so that we could eat dinner together. My mother had prepared dinner early in order not to get caught in the darkness bound to envelope the whole landscape once the rain stopped.

I peeped outside as I waited for my mother's reply. The rain was still raging on unabated and I briefly wondered what my father was doing in this storm, alone, and in the dark. The smoke still came from the heap of rubbish in the backyard which we had weeded from the gardens that afternoon and I also wondered how this fire had survived in all this storm.

This heap of rubbish would soon turn into ashes and later, my mother would plant green vegetables in it which she would sell in the nearby market. The storm outside was becoming stronger and my mother went to the corner of the kitchen and got a palm-leaf which hung on the soot-covered wall. The priest had poured holy water on this palm-leaf on the last Palm Sunday and my mother believed it was blessed. She threw it in the raging storm and it miraculously abated.

When it became apparent that my father was not going to join us for supper, my mother decided to serve us. She wanted us to go in the main house where we would be warm and secure. She had still not answered my question but continued to tell us stories which both frightened and excited us. My cousin, who was also my best friend, was around having come to spend the weekend with us. My mother told us a story of a legendary thief who once lived in our village long before were born.

"This man's name was Buchachi and he was known across the ridges and valleys for his bravery when it came to stealing," my mother began.

"Everyone loved and respected him, for even if he was a thief, he had great respect for fellow villagers and as a rule, never stole from them. Whenever he went on his missions outside the village, he would come back with lots of things. He would distribute them evenly to the villagers. Children who had been sent out of school, people whose loved ones were in prison and hospitals or those whose stock was dwindling in stores, would all come to this man for help and he would solve their problems. But of course, he was unpopular among the security organs, to say the least. Whenever they set out to arrest him, no one was willing to offer any useful information or they would even alert him of the policemen's presence and he would manage to escape. Another big problem was that no one, among the security officials, knew what this man looked like. There were also unconfirmed reports that he was capable of switching identities whenever he was in trouble. The police was baffled and did not know what to do. So they decided to bribe one of his best friends and use him. This friend agreed to betray Buchachi and hand him over to the police. He lured him to his house one night and as agreed, the policemen came at the appointed time.

Buchachi, being the thief he was, immediately sensed danger when he heard muffled voices outside. He knew it was useless to try and escape, so he waited calmly for whoever was outside to come and arrest him. As soon as the policemen entered, he stood up and said, 'Here he is at last, when do I collect my reward for handing you the most notorious thief in the century?' The other man was too surprised to say anything, and as he struggled to break the grip of the policeman and deny that he was not the thief, Buchachi escaped!"

"What happened then, mother?" I asked, fascinated.

"Well, the police knew that they had been duped. But that man never survived the wrath of the villagers. They lynched him to death. As for Buchachi, he was never seen again in the village."

The story ended and we all went in the main house to sleep. Outside, the wind was rustling through the many trees which littered our compound, turning the wet night into a cold one.

When my father finally returned, he was drunk as usual and I heard his drunken insults as he abused my mother. She kept quiet as she always did on such occasions, not wanting to trigger off another quarrel with him. He demanded for his dinner, which of course had gone cold and my mother dutifully brought it. He tasted a few mouthfuls and declared that it was tasteless. He then called me and asked me to dance as he ate, which I did obediently. He continued to stuff food in his mouth and munch away until he had finished all the food on the plate.

It was a great wonder that I did extremely well in class despite the tense environment I was living in at home. My father continued to treat me as if I were a piece of cow-dung and constantly hit me whenever he had an excuse, or even when he did not have one. I was like his punching bag.

I still remember one ghastly incident which occurred around the time I was twelve years. My father was going to visit his brother and I had wanted to go with him because I wanted to play with my cousin who was my age mate and best friend. He told me sternly that he would not go with me, but I insisted and began following him. When he turned and saw me on his heels, he picked a big stone, and with all his energy, hurled it at me.

"Go back, you bastard," he shouted at me. There was a glitter in his eyes which I had never seen before. It was a mixture of anger and hatred. I stood there, tears of frustration rolling down my cheeks. I meekly went back home and narrated the sad incident to my mother. She did not make any comment but I could see that she was greatly disturbed. I was lucky that I had dodged the stone, otherwise, I would have been dead meat.

When I was fifteen years, my mother called me aside and told me why she thought my father treated me so.

"When you were born, he denied having fathered you. He claimed that I had got you from somebody else."

I stared at my mother for a long time, not knowing what to say.

"What is the truth mother?" I asked with a lot of difficulty.

"My son, I would never lie to you. You are your father's son."

She said this without shifting her gaze and I knew she was telling me the truth. It did not help me to know the truth because I was powerless to do anything. I thought of confronting my father, but what good would it do? He still paid my school fees despite everything and at the moment, that was more important than anything else. With this disturbing knowledge, my relationship with my father continued to deteriorate. I couldn't imagine where he had got that crazy idea that I was not his son. I tried to compare myself with the rest of my siblings, and found no big difference. Even the teachers at school said that I resembled my cousin, and this was my father's brother's son.

I asked my mother if she could justify my father's claims. She told me that it was because I did not have the protruding chin which was like a birthmark in his clan. I could not see how this had alarmed my father. I was naturally a fat boy and the baby fat around my cheeks was still visible. So how could one tell if I was going to have the protruding chin or not.

I finished my secondary level and passed well. I was admitted to higher secondary school and I had to leave home to go to another town. It was a welcome interlude in my life, but I missed my mother immensely. I knew she was the only person who really cared for me. My relationship with my siblings was strained. I knew they had heard of the rumour that I was not their real brother from our neigbours who talked about it quite openly.

I spent the two years it took to complete my higher level without gong back home. I had promised myself never to go back until I joined university so that I would not have to ask my father for school fees. But I was summoned back when my mother was on her death bed and wanted to see me.

I broke down when I saw my mother's emaciated body lying in bed. My elder sister told me that she had a miscarriage and lost a lot of blood and had no proper treatment. I hugged my mother's frail body and she clung to me as if I had come to save her. I blamed myself for not checking on her regularly.

"I...wanted...tell...you something..." my mother started to say but the effort was too much for and she began gasping for breath. She could not continue. The following day she died. I was devastated and left soon after the burial. I could not see how I would ever step in that house again because there seemed to be no reason to.

For five years, I lived without hearing anything from what used to be my home, and truthfully, I was not bothered. I had got a good job and moved to the city. Occasionally, I did get a letter from my elder sister telling me what was happening at home, but that was all. I never bothered to write to my father and for all I knew, he never missed me.

Then one day, I was at the bus park where I had gone to meet my sister from the village. She was with a man who looked haggard and rather sickly. When they drew nearer, I realised that it was my father. I was momentarily shocked by his appearance and why my sister had not told me that she would be coming with him. She had only said that she was coming to the city for treatment.

"Good evening," I said to him.

He turned to me, startled. It seemed as if he had not expected to find me here.

"Do I know you?" he asked, surprised.

I knew he was not pretending. We had spent almost seven years without seeing each other and I must have changed a lot in that time. I said nothing. He took a few steps towards me and his eyes seemed to have registered some recognition. He opened his mouth to say something, then closed it again. His lower lip began to quiver, then fell. His eyes bulged, as if they would pop out. I noticed beads of perspiration on his forehead which slowly began trickling down until they settled on the tip of his nose. He took another step and this time stood directly in front of me. He reached out with his hands and began tracing the contours of my chin as if he wanted to commit it to memory.

"You are my son," he whispered, tears glistening in his eyes. "My true son."

"Yes," I answered. "I'm your son, Richard... Richard Kalenzi."

Those Days in Iganga

Regina Amollo

"It talked," Lilian said. "It told the truth," she added ready to burst into laughter.

"Oh, Lilian!" Rose exclaimed bursting into laughter.

They laughed as they entered Iganga Hospital where they worked as nurses. When they saw the sister-in-charge standing in front of the Maternity Ward, they stopped laughing and nudged each other with smiles and parted.

Rose worked in the Female Ward which was next to the Male Ward where Lilian worked. Both wards were full of patients, mainly suffering from sleeping sickness (mongota). The work started with reading the report, handing over to the in-coming nurse on duty and then going through the tedious task of greeting patients. Nurse Rose found these greetings tedious because she had never seen or known people who had lengthy greetings as the Basoga did! Those people could greet you for more than twenty minutes. Asking you about everything, I mean about everything; your husband, sister, children, the chicken, one of which might have been given to you by one of them! They were very generous.

By the time Rose reached the end of the ward, she would be tired but she would try to smile as best as she could since all she knew were the answers to those greetings and a few other words of Lusoga. She was from Soroti. By the way, greetings continued throughout the day, because whenever Nurse Rose went to a patient to take her blood pressure count, the patient would thank her again and again and start the greetings afresh. Some of these patients, after being discharged, would come back with gifts for Nurse Rose when they came for check-ups. They would bring her fresh maize, beans, ripe bananas and pawpaws. These days they call it corruption or bribery but in those days, it was the way people expressed their gratitude for the care given to them while in the hospital.

After work, Lilian collected Rose and they left for their single shared rooms in the staff quarters behind the hospital.

"It talked," Lilian said again, amused and she looked at the overgrown grass around the hospital fence.

"Do you expect to see another one?" Rose asked.

"You can never know," Lilian answered. "Do you think that woman in the garden expected to see that tortoise? And yet there it was, talking to her."

"I would have collapsed if I were her," Rose said.

"You would not," Lilian said. Africans rarely collapse. The worst thing that would have happened to you would have been for your hair to stand on end like *Ekanya's* and your eyes to bulge until they almost popped out in disbelief," Lilian said, laughing.

"But really," Rose insisted, "what did you say exactly happened?"

"It is a long story. Let us get out of these uniforms first and make some tea. Then while we seep our sugarless tea, I will unfold to you the 'truth, nothing but the truth' as told by the tortoise."

So after they had changed, bathed, put some beans on the fire to cook, they sat down on a mat to take the sugarless tea, because in those days, sugar was hard to come by, 'essential commodity', it was called then. But Lilian surprised Rose by producing some in a small tin.

"Honestly, how did you get it?"

"Connections, my dear. I was connected to Mr Isabirye by my patient. Mr Isabirye knows someone, who knows someone at the boarder and this one at the boarder is the one who buys and sells it through the same channels. So as it moves from hand to hand, it also gets less and less, TRANSPORT, they call it my dear. So can you believe this is supposed to be a kilo? Yes, because of transport. May be these days they call it VAT. I know you want to hear so much about the tortoise story."

"Yes." Rose was ready to laugh as Lilian's stories were always funny.

"Do you know that old man called Kinaule who sells ripe bananas across the road?"

"Of course. Get on with the story," Rose said impatiently.

"His daughter is the one the tortoise talked to. She is called Robinah, married two years ago but up to now, she has not got a child. So she went and consulted a witchdoctor who advised her to mix her husband's blood with some other man's to warm it up, implying that her husband's was cold which made it impossible for her to get pregnant. Her husband, Mr Waiswa, is a *kase* smuggler so she got the opportunity when he left for Busembantya to buy *kase*."

"Interesting," Rose remarked.

"Well, Robinah, Mrs Waiswa, had got her *mixer* called Musa who is a butcher. They agreed to meet near the cassava garden where Robinah was weeding at 11.00 am because by then the sun would have dried the dew from the grass. As Robimah pretended to be busy, she kept her ears alert for any movement or noise which would indicate that the *mixer* had arrived.

'Eh-hem,' she heard a sound like that of a man clearing his throat. She straightened up and looked about but there was nothing. Then she bent down again and inspected the garden of cassava but still she could see nothing. The sun was beginning to get hot.

'I'm here,', the voice said clearly. It was a man's voice but not Musa's.

As she looked about, she saw a tortoise crawling towards her saying, 'I'm here, let us talk.'

'Mama!' Robinah wailed, gathering her *gomesi* above her knees ready to take off.

'Don't run,' the tortoise warned. Robinah started to shake, her teeth chattering.

'Where is your husband? Take me to him,' the tortoise said.

'My husband...' Robinah began and swallowed bad saliva from a drying mouth. Then she saw Musa coming. 'Oh, Musa, come and see and hear this,' Robinah said, seeing Musa as her saviour.

'What is it?' Musa asked, seeing that she was really in a bad state. She was crying and shivering in spite of the hot sun. He thought that she might have been bitten by a snake or something, so he hurried over to her.

'Take me to the police station,' said the tortoise.

Jesus! Musa's hair stood on end. He grabbed Robinah's hoe so that he could crash the shell of the terrible talking tortoise but suddenly his hand became numb and he felt pain in his shoulder coming down to his hands. He dropped the hoe.

'Put me in that basket and let us go home where we can get a bicycle. I have to reach the Police station today,' the tortoise went on.

Musa got the basket which Robinah had brought for taking in some cassava home and lifted the tortoise and put it there. As he did this, the pain in his arm stopped. Now he was really frightened. He knew at once that he was dealing with a very powerful *mayembe* - evil spirit.

When they reached Musa's home, he wanted to take it inside where it would not be seen by anybody dropping in but the thing said, 'No, I want to sit under the tree'. There was an orange tree in front of the house and at the edge of the compound. Robinah had no more words. She just got her hoe and left. The tortoise did not mind her leaving; it wanted the company of a man like itself.

Musa had no bicycle so he told the tortoise that he was going to borrow one.

'Make sure you come back. If you don't, I leave it to you to guess what is likely to happen'. Musa guessed that he would drop dead somewhere if he refused to come back.

Musa found his friend, Paulo, making a lot of noise as usual, flattening tins for making *tadobas* - 'small tin kerosine lamps'.

'Paulo, can you lend me your bicycle now?'

'What is the matter? You have not even greeted me,' Paulo complained.

'It is urgent, I will tell you about it when I come back from Iganga Police station.

'Eh, man what is happening?' Paulo asked. Musa was sweating. He looked wild with uncombed hair. His shirt tails were hanging out of his trousers and there was a harassed look on his face.

Paulo entered his small house and rolled the bicycle out and gave it to Musa without another word. Musa grabbed it, jumped on it and disappeared. Paulo watched him and shook his head.

At home, Musa found the tortoise where he had left it, under the cool shade of the orange tree. He lifted the basket where it was and tied it to the bicycle carrier. Then he went off to the Police station.

He arrived at the station around 4.00 pm. Constable Kato and Otim were at the counter talking about the best way to trap *Kase* smugglers. The President rewarded any Police officer who arrested *kase* smugglers. They were still at it when they saw a man lean his bicycle against the wall of the building, untie a piece of luggage and come towards them with it. Musa put the tortoise on the police counter and went back to his bicycle as if to put it in a shade. As soon he was out of sight of the policemen, he jumped on his bicycle and fled.

'Take me to Kampala,' the tortoise said. 'I want to talk to the President.'

The two police constables could not believe their eyes and ears. They grabbed their rifles but their arms became numb and they could not shoot. So they put their guns down and went to look for a car to take the tortoise to Kampala.

When they were ready to go, the tortoise talked again.

'I want to sit in front with the driver.'

Otim had gone out to look for the man who brought the tortoise but he was no where to be seen. People gathered in front of the Police station. Women, men and children, all came to see the talking tortoise. They shook their heads in disbelief while others found the spectacle amusing. The tortoise was put in the front seat and taken to Kampala. Up to now, no one knows what happened to it after that. But it talked and told the truth," Lilian concluded mischievously

"Goodness, that was quite a story."

"Yes, it happened around 1976 and by the way, some smart journalist picked up the story and published it in the newspaper. For one week, the news was ' President Amin, Dr, DSO, IMC, said that anyone found talking about...' Actually I don't know if it was really on the radio because as you know, I don't have one. May be it was made up to make people laugh.

Becoming a woman

Hilda Twongyeirwe

Sex was an unutterable word in our homestead. Speaking any word connotative of sex meant a slap in the face, a beating on the buttocks, a bang on the head or a stare that could send a cold shiver down the spine. This particular day was a disaster for me. I was only twelve years old, a timid small girl. I did not know what to do neither did I have the courage to ask my mother, my father or friends about the unhurting wound between my legs. Anything between the legs was unuterrable. Why? We did not know. Was it sacred? Taboo? Dirty? There was never an explanation. It was just 'don'ts' and 'nevers' that were always slapped into our faces.

It was a hot afternoon when my three friends and I decided to go swimming in a shallow stream behind the school. We threw off our uniforms and tucked our underwears into our uniform pockets, then jumped into the water. The teachers prohibited this swimming, saying that there were many harmful insects in the water. This always amused us because every Wednesday afternoon, the teachers herded all the dirty pupils to this very river and forced them to bathe there. Sometimes the teachers would actually fold their trousers and step into the water to 'help' scrub the dirty rogues using rough stones.

Once in the cool waters away from the sharp rays of the hot sun, none of us realised that we had spent almost an hour there. It was coming to 4.00 pm. Which was the time for Art and Crafts. That meant some pupils were coming down to the river to soak and soften their ropes and fibres for use in their handiwork. It was then, that we heard some voices from some distance away. We jumped out of the water and in panic grabbed our clothes. That was when I saw stars.

When I pulled my knicker out of my uniform pocket, it had red stains! I examined my hands wondering whether something had just cut me while in the water but there was no wound. And the stain was not wet. I was scared. Had someone messed our things while we were in the water? But we had left them in sight and we had not seen anyone near them. We no longer dared to leave our clothes out of sight because one day, a mad man had come, picked them and disappeared with them. We had been forced to stay in the river till it had become dark enough for us to dash home in total shame and embarrassment. Thank God we were very young then!

Quickly, I slipped on my uniform and tucked the knicker back into the pocket. My friends had already finished dressing. Two of them, Mbambale and Bakyoruganda dashed off. Meanwhile, the voices that had alerted us out of the water were drawing nearer.

"Eee!" Kyomuhendo grunted. "Finish dressing and we go."

"I have finished," I said.

"Your...your... what have put in the pocket?"

"My things."

"Put it on and we go," she insisted.

"Did did you see it?" I asked, worried that she had probably seen what I had been looking at.

"See what?" she also asked.

"What I have put away."

"I thought it was your knicker."

"Yes it is. I will put it on at school in the latrine," I answered.

"Let's go then," she said dashing off like a frightened cat. I followed suit but my heart was in the pocket. Just a few metres away, we met the pupils coming to the river.

At school, I felt a strong urge to tell my friend, Kyomuhendo, what I had seen but somehow I did not. Instead, I went to the latrine, looked at the thing again and started examining my body, from the knees to the *sacred wound*. There was no pain, but there was blood!

'I must be sick. Very sick,' I spoke aloud. 'Something must have hurt me deep inside,' I thought. Yes, there was no pain but I knew it would soon start. From the amount of blood on the knicker, and the fresh blood still coming, I imagined there was a huge wound! I shuddered. I wished it was a nose bleed because with that, I could easily show anybody and get help.

So many thoughts reeled through my head and I didn't know what to do. How could I dare tell anyone that blood was coming out of me through that place! How?

I thought of going to the school senior woman, but she was such a rude one. Since the dispensary was far from the school, about two miles away, I decided to go home, brave it and tell *Taata* about it. Of course I would not tell him everything. *Taata* used to keep some drugs at home and I knew he would help me, at least to cool the situation.

From the latrine, I went to the tree in front of our class. This was where we used to keep our mats for handiwork. Most girls had already removed theirs. I removed mine, took it to Kyomuhendo and asked her to keep it for me for a little while.

"Where are you going?" she asked.

"I am here," I said.

"Then stay with your mat and let's weave," she answered.

"I said stay with it for a little while, didn't you hear me?"

"Teacher Gringer is about to reach here. If you have forgotten his grinding stone of a hand, continue dragging yourself," she warned.

I did not answer back. I put the paper bag I used as my school bag on Kyomuhendo's mat and walked away. Without books and a mat, no one suspected that I was escaping. Behind the P7 class, the fence had a hidden outlet which so far no teacher had discovered. Soon, the school saw my back and in a few minutes, I was at home.

Under the mango tree in front of our kitchen, I found both my parents seated. *Taata* was listening to the radio while *Maama* sat on a black sack. It had been blackened by both age and by the ash with which she used to put sorghum in the sacks. She would then put the sacks full of sorghum under water for a day and night. After that, she would remove the heavy sorghum, of course with the help of men's strong hands. That was why our sacks were usually black.

Taata was seated on a three-legged stool. It was his special stool, covered with a leopard skin. Nobody else ever sat on it except my brother. Once I asked *Maama* why she never sat on it and she said that it was simply for men. She warned me sternly never to sit on it. "The day you sit on it will be the last day you will ever see your father again," she had said.

"Where will he go?" I had asked.

"He will die," she had answered with such seriousness that I could not question her again.

How could I, therefore, ever dare be the cause of my own father's death! Our neighbour had died recently and I had not forgotten the day and nightmare I had gone through. I hated death. I never sat on that stool and it almost symbolised death in my life. Yes - a death of some kind.

Seeing them seated there, I didn't know how to start narrating my ordeal. Their faces showed that they were talking about something very serious. I moved closer to greet them but before I did, they both asked me what was wrong. I kept quiet, biting my lips in confusion and shame.

"Is it time yet?" *Maama* asked.

"No, *Maama*."

"Are you sick?" *Taata* joined in.

"No...Yes...No," I faltered and started scratching the ground with my big toes.

"Are you sick? Your father is asking," *Maama* said.

"No!" I answered timidly but my heart was screaming a very deafening 'yes'.

"What had you come to steal? You thought we were not yet home so you came to steal and fill your pockets with sorghum and sugar!" *Taata* accused me falsely. Well, sometimes I used to steal some sorghum and eat it at school with my friends, but today I had surely not come for that.

"Why have you come home at this time and where are your books?" he pursued.

"What about your mat? Isn't today Wednesday? This girl! You also want to become like Makare's daughter who has made her parents close their lips in shame!" *Maama* said.

"That is how they start!" *Taata* added. "They crawl before they run."

"I am not feeling well, that is why I came home," I answered.

"I am not feeling well," *Maama* mimicked. "Is it the head, the stomach, the leg, or what? You come running and then start pretending that you are not well."

"*Maama*, it is the stomach," I said. "It is sick."

"She might be sick, you help her," *Taata* said as he got up and walked into the house.

"What is it? Girls your age are not supposed to be *sick* in the stomach," *Maama* said. "By the way, how old are you?"

"I don't know. Which year was I born?" I asked.

I sat down next to her, and started helping her shell the peas. *Maama* was not sure of the year in which she produced me but she still remembered the season. It was when they were harvesting sorghum. She had had a bad day in the fields and in the evening, when they were going back home carrying loads of sorghum, I struggled hard to come out.

"You wanted to reach home on your own," she said smiling. "So somewhere near Bashasha's home, I knelt down and produced you."

"You mean it was as easy as that?"

"Ho! Nyamihanda, Nyamihanda my child, you gave me pangs and knives, but not as much as your brother. Your brother almost killed me!" she said, her face contorted. I looked at her sadly and did not ask more.

"You said you were sick in the stomach," she continued after a while.

"Yes," I said as I got up, intending to go to the urinal to re-examine myself before telling her where I was sick.

But I did not need to. Everything had already explained itself. *Maama* called me back and handed me a piece of cloth from her shoulders. She used such pieces of cloth as veils against wind and cold. To her, moving without such a piece of cloth made her feel naked.

I didn't know why she was giving me her cloth, so I asked her whether she wanted me to take it into the house for her. She shook her head and told me to wrap it round my small body over the uniform. "Your uniform has become dirty," she said. I pulled the dress looking for the dirt and it was indeed there!

"Go to the bathroom and bathe. As soon as you finish, come and I will tell you what to do next," she said.

Suddenly I burst into tears. Heavy tears rolled down my cheeks and blinded me. She had seen it all. *Maama* got up from the black sack, put her hands on my shoulders and soothingly told me to stop crying.

"You are a very lucky girl," she said. "Every woman is supposed to see this but some do not - the unlucky ones. What has happened is a sign that you will bear children in future. It happened to me and that is how I managed to produce you. It happened to *Mukaka*, my mother, and that is how she was able to produce me and her other children. It has happened to all women who have children. Now that it has started, it will be happening to you every month for about three days. It is symbolically called 'going to the moon', *'okuza mu kwezi'*. And it means you are no longer a child but a woman.

"When you become a woman, you stop playing with boys of your age or older ones. They have also become men in a way. If you ever play with them, you will become pregnant. You will not see this blood again for nine months, after which you will produce a child. Young women who are not yet married are not supposed to produce and when they do, it is a curse to them and a big shame to their families." She paused and looked at me. "You must, therefore, stop playing with boys and men. It must be only your husband - the man you will get married to, who will touch you and give you beautiful daughters and sons." She took a deep breath and continued, "My child, you must try to hide this blood as much as possible. It is a private happening and every clean woman makes sure that she sees it alone. For example, have you ever seen mine?"

As if to reply, my sobs which had died down started all over again and *Maama* said, "Now go to the bathroom and find me in your room after you have finished bathing."

When I came out of the bathroom, *Maama* was seated on my bed. Beside her were small pieces of white cloth, cut into almost the same size. She instructed me on how to use them and left. I had become a woman. That night I tried to recall everything *Maama* had said to me. Much of it I had not quite understood but had not had the chance and the strength to ask.

At school, I did not try to live an isolated life but found myself alone most of the time for some days. As I looked at other girls, I wondered how many were already going through it. And how were they managing not to play with boys? Maama had not told me lies. I remembered all the girls in our village who had got pregnant. All of them had been driven out of their homes as if they had never belonged there! I did not want to ever go through the same ordeal and so I swore to play with girls only. This promise I kept for a few weeks. It was not like me to stop playing with boys. After a short while, I was already up the trees with boys, back to my former life style.

A number of days slipped by and soon I realised that almost two months had elapsed since I was 'in the moon'. *Maama* had said that I would be going 'into the moon' monthly. Then I recalled that she had also said to me, "You are a woman. You must never play with boys. If you do, your stomach will become large and round and you will produce a child. This will be a curse on you and a big shame to your family." I had not listened to her.

Without much force, my life style changed. I again stopped playing with boys and hoped and prayed that I was not already pregnant. But God was not on my side. Three months, four months, my God! My stomach started feeling funny. I was sure that I was pregnant. Every evening I got home, I threw off my uniform and examined my stomach. I did not look big but it surely felt bigger than it looked. I knew my eyes were playing me tricks of wishful thinking.

Seven months dragged by and I was more than confused. I had to tell someone. But who? *Maama*? Kyomuhendo? My brother? Who? I was going to die. I wanted to die. I wished I was dead! I resolved to tell Kyomuhendo. I would ask her not to tell anyone else. She was a year or two older than me but she was my closest friend at school and in the village. However, I never told her. By six months, some people were complaining that I was losing weight.

"She is growing up!" *Maama* would tell them. "As children grow up, they lose weight." I wished she knew what kind of growing up I was undergoing!

Then one day as we were walking back home from school, we noticed boys giggling behind us. They were pointing at us and there was no doubt that they were talking about us. I was with Kyomuhendo. She charged at them with a torrent of words but they laughed harder. Then I saw it, her dress, it was stained red! Just like mine had been the day *Maama* gave me her piece of cloth. My heart missed a beat and I stood still. When the boys had passed by us, I called Kyomuhendo and told her. She did not look as startled as I had anticipated.

"Has this happened to you before?" I asked her.

"You mean staining the dress? No, never," she said.

"No. I mean the blood. Is it happening to you for the first time?"

"No. Several times so far."

"You never told me!" I said accusingly.

"No."

We fell silent for sometime. Then she asked me to lend her my sweater. I did and she tied it around her waist, letting it fall over her spoilt skirt.

"These boys are fools," she said. "They laugh over silly things. Now tell me what were they laughing at? As if their mothers do not see monthly blood!"

Without any warning, I found my lips saying, "I am pregnant."

"What?" Kyomuhendo shouted, confusion, anger, sympathy, written all over her face.

So I told her. I told her everything right from the beginning. When I had finished, she held my hand and quietly asked, "Which boy has made you pregnant?"

"I don't know," I replied earnestly. "I have played with so many boys that I cannot tell which one it is."

She let go of my hand and shouted, "But why have you allowed boys to sleep with you when your mother warned you against it! You are such a fool."

"Who said anything about sleeping with boys?" I asked reproachfully, tears rolling down my cheeks. I hated myself for having poured out my heart to her. Why had I trusted her and sought her sympathy and advise! I bit into my lower lip and before I realised it, was bleeding. My friend kept quiet for sometime staring at me.

Then she came closer and said, "I am sorry." I kept quiet. "I am sorry, I didn't mean to hurt you." But she had hurt me and I cried without stopping.

"Please tell me, Nyamihanda, what games have you been playing with these boys?" she asked.

"All sorts!" I screamed through my flood of tears. "Climbing trees, wrestling, football, throwing buttons, all sorts of games!"

She kept quiet again and then asked, "Did you see your period only once - the first time only?"

"Yes."

"And since then you have not seen anything again?"

"No," I shook my head.

Then she laughed. I cried. She laughed so much that tears started running down her face. I pushed her aside and ran away. I ran and ran till my legs ached and she caught up with me. She held my shoulders and still laughing said, "You are not pregnant."

"I have not asked you," I said.
"You are not pregnant."
I kept quiet. Then she explained.

The fate of an expensive wedding

Margaret Ntakarimaze

It began when Joshua gave Mutume an engagement ring. Immediately after the party, Joshua reminded Mutume not to expose the ring to her father who was against their marriage. Bidding him good bye, she rushed home to her mother. While Mutume was narrating the event to her mother, Kakuru, her step brother, tiptoed to the kitchen door to find Mutume happily showing her mother the ring. He dashed out to inform his father what he had seen and heard.

Mzee Kyondo got hold of his walking stick and rushed home only to find that Mutume and her mother were quietly grinding millet. Without the usual greetings, he summoned them to a special meeting. Mother first, followed by daughter, entered the sitting room and sat quietly awaiting the expected explosion. They did not have to wait for long. He glanced at his wife first, and then at his daughter, then biting his lips said,

"You are both well aware that it is only me who makes decisions in this house" He paused, lit his pipe, and as he was about to continue, his eldest son, Mbwine entered.

Mbwine immediately realised that something unusual had taken place within the family. As he waited for his father to continue, he asked Mutume to bring him something to drink.

"My son," continued Mzee Kyondo, "I want you to pay close attention to what I am saying. Your sister, Mutume, is engaged to Joshua. I have learnt from a reliable source that she has just come from a party where she was given an engagement ring. This, I am not against but what I don't want is your mother making decisions for me when I am still alive."

It was at this point that Mutume entered with a glass of water for her brother and a calabash of sorghum porridge for her father.

Pretending not to notice her entrance, her father roared like a lion crossed, "If Joshua does not pay two million shillings and ten cows, Mutume will not be his bride."

On hearing this, Mutume ran out of the room.

"Father," his son calmly said, "you should not demand for so much."

Mzee Kyondo retorted loudly, "You don't understand, do you? I want to have an expensive wedding for my daughter. The best wedding there has ever been, with lots to eat and drink and with lots of people too."

Mutume's mother opened her mouth as if to speak, hesitated, then braved on, "Father of my children, we should be careful. Making expensive weddings for our children has resulted in their marrying when they are either too old or outside the church. I had planned a simple wedding for Mutume. I wanted them to be united by the pastor and those who would like to come and witness it without being attracted by a party would be welcome. A simple wedding, I am sure, would do, to avoid them starting married life in debt."

"There you are again, making decisions for me in my home," retorted Mzee Kyondo. "Since when did a woman decide for her husband? Your role is to look after the children. When they grow up, like Mutume has now, we, the men discuss bride wealth to be paid for them without interference. Do you mind going back to your grinding stone? In any case, I expected supper to have been served by now. I will ensure that my daughter gets married to a rich man who can pay me all I want, whatever your feelings."

At this point, Merab got up and walked slowly back to the kitchen without glancing back. She could not bear his scorn. On seeing his mother leave, Mbwine followed her unnoticed. He tried to sooth her.

"Mother," he said, "our pastor, too advises people to have simple weddings. Instead of having thousands of people attend your wedding and spending all your savings, you can have just a few people. After all, the idea is to have witnesses. By doing this, you can spend the rest of the money on building your home."

"My son, you are right," his mother interjected. "Unfortunately, to the majority of the people, weddings mean feasting."

"By the way, where is Mutume?" Mbwine asked his mother. "Mutume, Mutume!" her mother called. There was no response. They looked everywhere, but she was nowhere to be found. Suddenly, Mzee Kyondo came out with a torch. Rushing to the road leading to Joshua's home, he swore, "You are a dead man, Joshua, if I find Mutume with you. You too, Mutume."

To his disappointment, Mutume was not there either. Joshua, knowing their hiding place, put on his coat and unnoticed, sneaked out. As expected, he found his bride-to-be there. She was crying. He reached for her, held her gently, whispering all the while that all would be well. On hearing this, Mutume stopped crying and narrated everything her father had said. Tactfully, Joshua changed the topic until there was a smile on her face. In a better mood, Mutume agreed to be taken home. However, before they bid each other farewell, they heard Mbwine whispering, warning Joshua to run for his life. Joshua ran home and Mutume was led back by her brother.

On reaching home, Mutume and her brother heard their mother yelling for help. They rushed to her rescue. They found their father gripping her throat. On seeing Mutume, Mzee Kyondo let loose his wife and charged towards his daughter. "There your are," he said. "Tonight, I am going to teach you that I am not to be angered." He got hold of her, led her into a room and locked the door. His son tried to dissuade him to no avail. Without a word, Merab brought a mat and mother and son kept vigil at Mutume's door all night long.

The following morning, Mzee Kyondo left home early. When he came back, he found many people gathered at his homestead. The women were wailing and the men had their spears' points down which, according to the traditions of their clan, indicated loss of a member of the family. He rushed to Mutume's room only to find her dead. Besides her body, was her mother weeping uncontrollably. Mzee Kyondo went outside. With tears running down his face, he stood before the gathering, and in a tone which reflected his deepest sorrow and shame said, "Fellow parents, relatives and friends, the fate of an expensive wedding has cost me my daughter. Merab, will you ever forgive me?" Then he looked heavenward and prayed.

AMOLLO Regina was born in Kaberamaido in North-Eastern Uganda. She attended Lwala St Mary's Girls' Primary School, Mt St Mary's College, Namagunga and Mulago School of Nursing and Midwifery. Later, Amollo specialised as a pediatric nurse and is currently working in Soroti Hospital. Her first novel, *A Season of Mirth* was published by FEMRITE Publications (1999). She enjoys writing fiction in her free time.

AYETA Anne Wangusa hails from Mbale district, Eastern Uganda. She went to Buganda Road Primary School, Mt St Mary's College, Namagunga and Makerere High School. She holds a Bachelor of Arts honours degree and a Master of Arts degree in Literature of Makerere University. She is currently working as a sub-editor with Uganda's leading daily newspaper, *The New Vision*. Her first novel, *Memoirs of a Mother*, was published by FEMRITE Publications (1998). She is working on her second novel.

BARENZI Lillian studied at Gayaza Junior, Gayaza High School and Makerere University where she did Mass Communication. She is a professional journalist who works for *The New Vision* newspaper as a creative writer and a runs a regular column, *Never Trust*. She also writes for various other magazines. Her interests include female reproduction issues and reading novels by Afro-American authors.

BARUNGI Violet works as an editor of *New Era* magazine. She holds a Makerere University Bachelor of Arts honours degree in History. Her publications include *Cassandra*, a novel published by FEMRITE Publications (1999), *Tit for Tat,* children's short stories (1997), *The Shadow and the Substance*, a novel by Lake Publishers (1998). Her play, *Over My Dead Body*, won the 1997 British Council International New Playwriting award for Africa and the Middle East Region. She has also published a number of short stories in magazines and short story anthologies.

DIPIO Dominic is a lecturer in the Literature Department at Makerere University. She studied at St Mary's College, Aboke and Trinity College, Nabbingo and holds a Bachelor of Arts with Education degree and a Master of Arts degree in Literature both of Makerere University. She is currently doing her PhD. Dipio writes short stories and plays. One of her plays, *The Sweet Yoke*, a religious play, has been produced and staged several times by the Comboni Missionaries. Her other play is, *The Irresistible Encounter*. She ha also written a biography of Bishop Caesar Asili which has been submitted for publication and is currently writing reflections entitled, *Come Back to Me*. She is interested in exploring gender issues and her writings reveal profound understanding of human nature.

KESHUBI Hope is currently the Programme Co-ordinator, Basic Education of Redd Barna- Uganda. She was born in Kabale, South-western Uganda. She holds a Diploma in Education and a Bachelor of Education degree of Makerere University and a Master of Education degree in Education of University of Exter. Her publications include: *Dissertation Writing- A Guide* published by New Expression Press (1995), *Going Solo,* a novel by Fountain Publishers (1997), *To a Young Woman*, a novel by Lukesh Educational Publications (1997) from where *Joannita's Nightmare* is extracted. She has written a biography of her late husband, Cliff Lubwa p'Chong, titled *Confessions and Professions* and her own autobiography titled, *In Search of Myself*, both to be published by Lukesh Educational Publications. She is now working on her third novel, *Lopsided Justice*. Keshubi is a humorous but blunt steadfast woman who will tell it to you straight. Her eyes perceive the ramifications of life in a unique way which she glaringly puts to print.

KIGULI Susan is a lecturer in the Literature Department at Makerere University. She holds a Bachelor of Arts with Education degree and a Master of Arts degree in Literature, both of Makerere University, and a Master of Literary Linguistics degree of the University of Strathclyde. Her collection of poems, *The African Saga,* was published by FEMRITE Publications (1998). Kiguli also writes short stories and some of them have been published in various magazines and journals in Uganda, UK and USA. Her writings reveal a keen sense of humour and a sharp eye for detail.

Notes on contributors

KYOMUHENDO Goretti is currently working as the Co-ordinator of FEMRITE. Her first novel, *The First Daughter,* was published by Fountain Publishers (1996) and it enjoyed immense popularity both in Uganda and abroad. Her second novel, *Secrets no More,* was published by FEMRITE Publications (1999). She has also written for children: *Different Worlds* published by Monitor Publications (1998). She is currently working on her third novel. She is an Honorary Fellow of Creative Writing of The University of Iowa- USA.

NABWERU Philo is a teacher of English Language and Literature in English. She holds a Bachelor of Arts degree in Literature and Psychology of Makerere University. She is interested in poetry and drama and the welfare of children and women. Some of her poems have been published in *Dhana*, a literary magazine of the Literature Department, Makerere University.

NTAKARIMAZE Margaret hails from Kisoro district, South-Western Uganda. She is a Business Administrator by profession. Her collection of poems, *Which Battle*, is in the process of being published. Some of her poems have been published in the *Monitor* and broadcast on Radio Uganda. She participated in the Okot p'Bitek Competition award in 1991 and her poem, *In Praise of Okot p'Bitek* was recited during the 1996 Makerere University Literature Festival. She is working on her second book.

TINDYEBWA Lillian was born in Rukungiri district, South-Western Uganda. She holds a Bachelor of Arts degree of Makerere University. Her first novel, *Recipe for Disaster* was published by Fountain Publishers (1994) and she is currently the General Secretary of FEMRITE.

TWONGYEIRWE Hilda was born in Kabale district, South-Western Uganda. She studied at Kacherere Primary School, Bishop's Girls' School Muyebe, Uganda Martyr's School Rubaga, National teachers College, Nkozi and Makerere University where she graduated with an honours degree in Social Sciences. Her poems appear in *New Horizons* and *Dhana* magazines. Her interest lies in creative writing, acting and reading.